Silenc

Diana Kurth

A run in with sexy Ryan Campbell, outside her mother's gift shop in the small town of Willowbrook, was the beginning of a major life change for Emma Jones.

Heartbreaking news that she receives from her mother that same day, has her searching in desperation for answers, and fate has it that Ryan is just the man to deliver what she needs.

Clouded by guilt, love, loss and mixed signals, they each struggle with the emotional rollercoaster they find themselves on.

Is love at first sight a real thing or is it just imagined?

Silence of the Night

A Holiday Romance Novel

Diana Kurth

1. Edition, 2022

Cover by All Kinds of Covers
Edited by Grace Augustine
Diana Kurth - Toronto, Ontario
author.dkurth@gmail.com
https://www.authordianakurth.com/

To Marilyn,

Thank you for the inspiration, kind words, and all your wonderful thoughts and suggestions. It is all truly valued. Your dedication to my writing is part of what keeps me going. Thank you for understanding my journey.

Love always.

Chapter 1

Emmalee Jones rested her arm on her desk, and glanced at her watch, wondering where her life had gone wrong. She used to dream of finding the perfect man, falling in love, marriage, family, but life for her didn't exactly go that way. Instead, she's been feeling like a recluse, not the vibrant, early-thirties woman in the prime of her life. And time seemed to stand still as she reflected on her boring life. She was going nowhere.

What happened to my life?

She looked out the window and cringed.

"I can't believe it's only three o'clock. It feels like the longest day ever, doesn't it?" Emma asked Nisha, who sat at the desk on the other side of the partition in front of hers. Nisha had been her assistant for the last four years and now a friend.

"I don't know what you're talking about," Nisha stated. "I think the day has just flown by."

"Are you kidding me? It feels like it should be around seven o'clock. Look outside. It's starting to get dark already."

"Girl, we go through this every year. It's time you accept that the days are shorter in the winter." Nisha chuckled.

"Yeah, but why does it feel like the days get longer instead?"

"Head down, dig into your work. I need to finish this up before the end of the day, remember? If you dig in, you won't even notice the time fly by."

"That's because it doesn't," Emma snickered and immersed herself into her work.

As a cost analyst, she spent a lot of time looking at numbers in spreadsheets. Emma had mastered excel databases and formulas. She had been with Radison Industries, a multinational manufacturing firm, for more than ten years and was a significant member of the team. She began working for the corporation before finishing her college courses because it was a once-in-a-lifetime chance, or so she thought at the time. She was starting to feel like there was more for her out there, someplace, ten years later, after getting halfway up the corporate ladder. "You got plans tonight?" she heard Nisha ask.

Looking up from her computer screen, she noticed several colleagues collecting their belongings, cleaning up their desks, putting on coats, and she glanced at her watch again. Amazed that it was five o'clock, she started to pull her own papers together, and had to admit, Nisha had been correct. Time did fly when you didn't pay attention to it.

"No, another boring Friday night," she replied, feeling the sting of realization.

Like usual.

"Why don't you come out with Patti and me? We're going to Everliegh's tonight. Come with us. I'm sure you could use a drink or two, right?" Nisha coaxed as she came around the partition. She was a petite young woman of Indian heritage, her skin the color of wheat and her eyes the color of semi-sweet chocolate. Her long, layered, dark brown hair colored with a few blonde streaks through it, flowed straight down her back. Her smile was wide, her teeth a brilliant white, and her cheeks slightly sunk in. She needed no makeup as her natural beauty shone through.

"Nah, I'm too old for nightclubs, and quite frankly, I don't have that kind of energy anymore," she laughed.

"How long has it been since you've been out?" Nisha asked.

Here we go again. I wish people would leave me alone about how I live. I'm fine, don't they see that?

"Oh, it's been a while, but nightclubs aren't my thing. The music is too loud. You can't even hear yourself think, let alone hear another person's conversation."

"Well, if you change your mind, you know where we are. I worry about you." Nisha gathered her coat and purse from the nearby closet, waving goodbye as she stepped out the door. "Have a good weekend," she called out.

Emma pondered for a second about why she hadn't been out on a date or simply out for drinks with friends in such a long time. She should be living life to the fullest at her age. She's now in her thirties and still waiting for that dream to come true but realizing at that moment that she was doing nothing to make it happen because she spent her time at home reading, painting, or watching television when she wasn't at work. It just became too easy to not have to dress up and make nice all the time.

You need to get out more. You're becoming a hermit. Next you'll turn into an old cat lady. Then you'll die alone.

The phone at her desk rang pulling her back to reality, and she stared at it wondering if she should answer as her watch showed 5:08 p.m.

Who the hell would call me at this hour on a Friday? Don't they know I have a life?

Then realizing she didn't have one anymore, she lifted the handset.

"Emma Jones," she stated then paused to listen.

"Emmie?"

"Mom? Is that you? Is everything alright?" No one but her mother called her Emmie.

"No dear," she heard from the other end. "I need to see you."

"I'll be there in a week mom. I'm coming home for Christmas, remember?"

"Emmie, this can't wait. I need to see you as soon as possible, please."

"What's wrong mom? Tell me what's going on," she said, suddenly feeling her anxiety build. Her mom never called her, asking her to come home. She knew that something was wrong.

"I'll tell you when you get here, sweetie. Please come. I need to talk with you."

"Alright, I'll drive out in the morning. Is that okay?"

"Yes, dear, that will be fine. Thank you, Emmie. I appreciate it. I know how busy you are."

"No problem, Mom. See you tomorrow. Love you." She replaced the handset, wondering what could be so important that it couldn't wait.

Emma felt a wave of shame sweep over her for not paying more attention to her mother, but that would have meant listening to her mother voice her need for her father over and over again. The man passed away three years ago and her mother still mourned him. As a result, she hadn't visited as much as she should have in the last couple of years. Mom had plenty of people to lean on, she had always reasoned.

She reached for her purse in her desk drawer and retrieved her jacket from the closet and looked back to make sure all was in order before stepping out the door. She attempted to put the guilt behind her as she walked to the elevator, but it nagged at her.

I guess I'll stay the weekend. That should make her happy.

Chapter 2

Emma set out at 7 a.m. for the three-hour drive north. It had snowed during the night leaving a blanket of two inches, making some of the streets that had not been cleared yet by the plows, a little treacherous. She was thankful that there wasn't much traffic, and when she merged onto the highway, the drive became easier. She turned on the radio and listened to the stylings of her favorite artists, singing along with them when she knew the words to distract her from the worry she felt about her mom's call.

Hours later, as she drove into the small town of Willowbrook, where her mother resided, she couldn't help but notice the amount of Christmas decorations that lined Main Street, the town's hub for shopping. Small holiday trees in large planter boxes on the sidewalks were draped with lights and decorations. Huge golden wreaths, each with an oversized red bow, hung from streetlamps that looked like lanterns hanging from a pole. Each store had their own distinctive Christmas window and the leafless trees that sprang from the sidewalks intermittently, were strung with golden lights that sparkled. The dusting of snow created an almost magical winter scene.

Wow. Straight out of the movies. Gets better every year.

She imagined how beautiful it must be at night with all the lights against the night sky. In the years she had visited her parents, she had never seen the street lit up at night.

Emma slipped into a parking spot beyond her mom's red-bricked gift shop, reasoning that her mom would be there as it was after 10 o'clock. She reached into the glove box and retrieved her spare pair of black leather gloves and put them on as she glanced around. She took off the glasses she wore for driving and set them on the dashboard, and pulled up the hood of her grey bomber jacket, grabbed her purse, and stepped out of the car, locking it remotely when she pushed the door closed.

As she rounded her black Mazda 3, her knee-high boots sank into the snow that was pushed up against the curb from the plows that had cleared the road earlier in the day. Once on the sidewalk, she stomped her feet a few times to help remove the snow from her boots, and walked to her mom's store, Giftable You.

There were a number of pedestrians walking the sidewalks on both sides of Main Street at this early hour. Christmas was around the corner, and it was one of the busiest times for her mom. Half of her mom's yearly income came from the three to four weeks leading up to the holidays.

The door of the shop, suddenly burst open as she reached for the handle, knocking her back and making her lose her balance. She could feel herself falling to the ground and put out a hand to stop the inevitable from happening by grabbing onto the man that had just flown through that door.

The man watched, in what seemed like slow motion, as the brown-eyed woman grabbed onto his jacket sleeve while falling backwards, pulling him to the ground on top of her. There was nothing he could do to stop it from happening. When they hit the ground, he looked at her, stunned.

In a complete state of embarrassment, he quickly stood up again. "My apologies. Are you all right?" he asked in a half laugh, reaching down to help her up.

No.

"You're in an awful hurry." Emma replied, angered at what had happened, brushing the snow off her jeans and the sleeves of her jacket when she was on her feet again.

"No, sometimes I just don't think." he responded. "Here, let me help you," he said, smiling as he brushed his hand down her back to get the snow off of it.

Get your hands off me.

"No, stop," she said loudly, stepping away from him, now a little more infuriated. "I'll be fine, thank you." She looked at the amused smile on his face. He had a comically crooked smile that suddenly moved her from being upset with the matter, to a position of seeing the hilarity in it. "Are you in a habit then of just barreling through doors?" she chuckled when she regained her composure. She noticed his steel-blue eyes that were framed by long, dark eyelashes, and laugh lines at the corners. He donned a slight 5 o'clock shadow on his square jaw. It wasn't a model handsome face like you see in the magazines, but there was enough appeal to capture her attention.

"Again, no, I wasn't looking, and didn't see you there. My apologies." He was busy brushing snow off his own clothes. He was studying her face, noticing her clear, creamy skin with a touch of pink on her cheeks. Her full lips formed a perfect smile, and she glowed.

"Well, thank you for helping me up. Have a good day," she said, trying to get around the almost six-foot frame that blocked the doorway.

"Let me make it up to you. Let me buy you a coffee, and we can get to know one another."

"I'd love to but I don't have the time." she responded trying once again to get around him.

Noting her impatience, he stepped out of the way, pulling the door open for her.

"Maybe another time," she said politely as she entered the shop, not noticing the hopeful look she had put on his face. "And watch where you're going!"

There were a few people browsing the various items in the store, and a woman behind the cash register that she didn't recognize. Her mother would normally be there. She glanced around to see if she could spot her mom and when she didn't see her, she approached the woman at the cash register who was finishing a transaction with a customer.

"Good day, can I help you?" she asked with a smile.

"Yes, I'm looking for Susan Jones. I'm her daughter." Emma replied.

"Your mom isn't in today. I've taken over for her for a while. I'm Katie Simmons." she said in a cold manner. "Why don't you head over to the house? You'll find her there."

Emma looked at the 50's something woman that turned her smiling face to a painful expression. She appeared tired, Emma thought. "Thank you, Katie. I'll do that." Emma replied, noting her cold manner.

Wonder what's got you ticked off?

She left the store, hopped back into her car and drove to her mom's house.

When Emma arrived at the house, she noticed that the Christmas lights hadn't been put up yet, and the snow on the driveway hadn't been cleared. She pulled up to the curb in front of the house, knowing that she'd have the task of shoveling later, and parked the car. Lifting her bag out from the trunk of the car, she walked up the drive, locking the car with that reassuring short beep she got from hitting the button on her fob. Emma discovered that the front door was locked when she tried to open it. She knocked a few times, but there was no answer. Her mom had given her a key, years ago which hung on her keychain, and she used it to get in.

"Mom?" she called out, putting her bag down. She removed her boots, placed them on the plastic mat beside the closet and hung up her jacket in the hall closet. Then grabbing the bag, she wandered further into the kitchen. There were no signs that her mom had been up yet.

She went up the carpeted stairs, and called out once more, "Mom?", receiving yet again no answer. She opened her mother's bedroom door, after knocking on it lightly, and found her mom sleeping on the bed under the burgundy comforter that she had gifted her last Christmas. Emma watched for a moment before putting her bag down and stepped into the room to give her mom a kiss on the cheek. She couldn't help but notice that her mother wore a sleep cap on her head and her face looked thin.

Something's definitely wrong here.

Her mother stirred a bit, and then opened her eyes, discovering her daughter next to the bed, smiling down at her.

"Mom, are you OK?" she asked in a soft voice.

"Yes, dear. I'm fine. I'm happy to see you." She wet her lips by running her tongue over them. "Why don't you go down and put on a pot of coffee, and I'll be down in a few minutes."

"Sure. Can I fix you something to eat?"

"A piece of toast might be nice, you fix yourself anything you want, though. I'm sure you haven't eaten."

Emma nodded and closed the bedroom door as she stepped out. She picked up her bag and carried it to the guest room where she would be spending the night.

Once down in the kitchen, the coffee brewed as she checked the fridge, and was taken aback to see how meagerly it was stocked.

You have nothing here to eat!

She looked in the breadbox and found a bag of bread that had six pieces left in it.

Probably stale.

She pulled out two slices, studied them carefully, and then popped them into the toaster, without pushing them down to toast.

When her mother arrived in the kitchen, fifteen minutes later, wearing her nightgown and bathrobe, Emma realized that she looked older than she remembered from her previous visit in May for her birthday. She looked ill as her skin was a pale grayish tone, she was very thin, and her body trembled with every motion she made. "Are you okay, Mom?" she asked with great concern.

"Sit down, dear, there are certain things that need to be discussed. Before we begin though, I'd love a cup of coffee and some toast," she responded, as she sat down at the kitchen table.

Emma observed that every movement that her mother made seem like it took great effort. She pushed the toast down and poured two cups of coffee, feeling deeply concerned now. "What would you like on your toast?" she asked.

"Just a bit of butter, and I take my coffee black now. There's no milk here, I haven't been able to get out to shop."

Seeing no butter, she got the margarine from the fridge and when the toast popped up in the toaster, she lightly slathered the two pieces and put the plate and coffee mug in front of her mother.

"I'll be happy to do some shopping for you. You'll have to make a list for me of what you want."

"That's kind of you. I'd appreciate it if you could, but we need to talk first."

Emma got her own mug of coffee from the counter and sat across from her Mom. "What's on your mind?"

"Emmie, I haven't wanted to worry you. You've been so busy for a long time now. But it's time I told you what's going on," she took a sip of her coffee, hands shaking while she lifted it to her mouth.

"What, Mom? You're scaring me." she said with growing concern.

"Well, dear, during a routine mammogram last January, I was diagnosed with breast cancer."

Emma gasped. "Why didn't you tell me?" she cried out, suddenly frightened.

"Like I said, I didn't want to worry you. This isn't my first go with it. I had breast cancer about 5 years ago. I had a lumpectomy done at that time, followed by chemo and radiation. I thought I was done with it. But, it has come back. This time, the cancer has moved to other parts of my body. I went through chemo and radiation again but it's very aggressive this time, they tell me."

No, this isn't happening. Please, God, this can't be.

Emma started to speak but she was cut off.

"Please, dear, let me finish. You can ask questions later. I just need to say it." She took a small bite from her piece of toast. Without looking up, she continued. "This time, I'm not so lucky. I have stage-four cancer and the treatments haven't been helping. It's spreading very quickly throughout my body. It's in my lymph nodes, my lungs, my bones, and my liver. The doctors have told me that I have only a short time to live and that I should get my affairs in order," she paused. "There, I said it. It's the first time I said it to anyone."

Now she looked up into Emma's eyes and saw the fear on her face and the tears forming.

"Why haven't you told me about any of this? I didn't know you had cancer 5 years ago. How did I not know?" she asked with tears streaming down her face.

"We didn't want to worry you. Your father was here to help me the first time around, bless his soul." Susan nibbled at her toast.

Raising her voice, Emma complained, "I'm your daughter. You should have told me back then and you should have told me when it re-occurred. You didn't have to go through all that you have alone. I had a right to know."

Susan placed her hand over Emma's and gave it a quick squeeze. "Dear, I wasn't alone. Your father was right there with me. I could feel his presence."

"I didn't even notice when I was here in May. Why didn't I notice?"

"Amazing what a good wig and makeup will do. I had a bit more energy back then, too."

"Mom, really, I could have helped. I would have gone to your treatments with you, shopped, cleaned house for you, cooked for you. You didn't have to do it alone."

"I had some friends come in now and again. Katie has been a big help at the store. She's run the store for about a year now."

"Well I'm here now and I'm staying. I'll do whatever I can to help you through this."

"You have your job, dear. I knew how busy you were and still are, but yes, now I could use the help. I wanted you to know so that when the time comes, you will know what to do. We'll talk about the will and such later." Finishing the last bit of coffee in the cup, she continued, "Right now, I think I'd like to go back up to bed and sleep a while longer. I get weaker every day. Are you settled in yet?"

You still should have told me.

"I dropped my bag in the guest room. I'll unpack later. Right now, I'll get you upstairs and then do a bit of shopping. You have no food here, Mom. You need to eat to keep up your strength."

"Alright, dear. If you wouldn't mind helping me upstairs, we will talk again later." As Susan tried to stand, Emma noticed her difficulty and helped her up.

It was a long, laborious climb up the stairs, and Emma deemed that her mother would never have to do that again. Once Susan was tucked back into her bed, Emma did a quick check through the house to see what was required from the store and made two lists, one for shopping and another for what needed to be done. She knew she had to talk to her mother's oncologist and that would be a priority for Monday. She needed to call Radison to inform them she was taking an indefinite leave of absence, maybe work her holidays in this year as she hadn't taken any. She would speak to Nisha, get set up to be able to work remotely when needed. She would talk to

Katie Simmons and see if she could give her any more information that her mom neglected to tell her.

Emma's focus was on getting things done and to make it easier for her mom, and she didn't have the time to wallow in grief. She wanted to make sure that her mom had the best possible life for whatever days she had left.

Chapter 3

Emma wandered through the aisles of the local grocery store, list in hand, selecting items she needed and placing them in the shopping cart. She tried to plan a few meals in her head as she made her way through the store, causing her to double walk some aisles. Being unfamiliar with the layout, she had trouble finding certain things that she required for those meals.

When she approached the deli counter for fresh luncheon meats, she spotted the same man that knocked her over earlier in the day.

Oh, gawd, not you again.

She took her place in the line, waiting for her turn, hoping he wouldn't remember her, and noticed that there were two more people ahead of her.

Hopefully, he won't notice me.

She pulled her phone from her jacket pocket, scrolled through her social media feeds, in an attempt to not pay attention. She didn't want another a conversation with him, she wasn't in the mood. Her priority was her mom right now.

"Well, hi there, didn't expect to see you here," came the familiar voice.

No such luck.

She put her phone away so that she didn't appear rude. "Hi, fancy meeting you here," she replied looking up at him and offering a half-grin. His blue eyes caught her attention as they appeared to be smiling. They seemed to sparkle.

"Look, I still feel awful about what happened earlier, let me buy you coffee so that I know you forgive me."

"I forgive you. You don't have to do that." she replied with a chuckle.

"Nah, if you don't have coffee with me, I'll take that as an indication that deep down you haven't forgiven me, and you're just being polite. Coffee shop is right next door," he said pointing in the direction.

"Well, what choice do you leave me then? Just a quick coffee, though, I really do need to get back home."

"Home? You live here? Why haven't I seen you here before?"

"Let's talk about that over coffee. I have to get this shopping done and back to the house as soon as possible. I'll see you next door in a bit. Is that alright?"

"Sure, if you promise you'll show up," he gave her that crooked smile that caught her attention earlier.

"Like I said, what choice do I have?" She pushed her cart forward a bit as the line moved.

"See you in a bit then." He rolled his shopping cart down an aisle.

She couldn't say no to Mr. Cute-with-the-crooked-smile. He did have a certain appeal. *Those eyes!*

She finished her shopping and pushed the cart full of groceries out to her car where she loaded the bags into the trunk. After returning the cart to the store, she walked towards the coffee shop. As she approached, she noticed him sitting in a booth at the window, watching her. She could see him start to jump out of the booth when she slipped and almost fell on the snow covered walkway, but with arms flailing and feet scrambling to catch her balance, she managed to recover like a trouper.

He waved as she entered, and caught her attention. "I've got your coffee for you," he smiled as she approached. "I hope you don't mind. You said you were in a hurry." The take-out cups of coffee sat on the table, his with the lid off, hers with packets of sugar and cream next to it. "I didn't know how you take your coffee," he stated apologetically.

She sat opposite him and pulled off her jacket. "Thank you. I appreciate that."

"My name is Ryan Campbell," he put out his hand over the table. "That was a great recovery by the way. I thought you were going down for a second time today," he smiled.

And both times because of you.

"Emma Jones," she responded, shaking his hand, feeling slightly embarrassed. "And if I had dropped, it would have been the second time you would have been the cause of it. I wouldn't have come this way if you hadn't insisted on buying me a coffee," she smirked as she put the cream and sugar into her coffee.

"True enough." Undaunted, he continued. "So, you're from here? Like I said, haven't seen you here before."

"No, my mom is here. I live and work in Toronto. Just visiting but home is always going to be where Mom is," she said with a nervous smile.

"I understand that. I grew up in the city and moved here. It just got too crowded there for me."

"How long have you lived in Willowbrook?" she asked.

"I drove through this town about 8 years ago and loved it. Decided then and there that this is where I wanted to be. I went to see a real estate agent, and he showed me the listing of the house that I'm in now. We went to take a look at it, it was empty and I bought it, same day. Went home, packed up and moved here."

"Wow, that's a quick move. My mom and dad love it here, too. Dad passed away a few years ago but mom won't move back to the city. She owns the Giftable You shop that you were in this morning." She sipped her coffee, hoping to finish it quickly so that she could return to her mom.

"Wait, that's your mom? She's a wonderful lady. I've spoken with her often. Haven't seen her in a bit, is she okay?"

Emma wondered how far she should go in this conversation while she sipped on her coffee. Deciding that it needn't get personal, she carried on in a general way. "She's been feeling a little under the weather. I'm here to help her out for a bit. Shopping, cooking, that sort of thing."

"Tell her I wish her a speedy recovery. If there's anything I can do to help, please, just let me know."

"And your family?"

"Oh, mom and dad are still in the city. They refuse to leave. Dad says he's got everything he needs there. The best hospitals in case anything happens, entertainment, he's a big baseball fan and can be found at the dome throughout the summer. He also has a small yacht in the harbor, so they go cruising around a lot. In the winter, they head south to the sunny beaches and spend a few months there."

"Wow, must be nice. So you're here alone? Not married?"

"Lost my wife 8 years ago. She was ill and never recovered. That's why I had to leave the city."

"I'm sorry to hear that. I understand." She took a sip of her coffee. "Look, I don't mean to be rude but I do need to get back to mom's. I have a driveway to shovel and groceries to put away. There's a bit to do because she hasn't been able to."

"Let me shovel the driveway for you. You focus on taking care of your mom."

Am I ever going to be rid of you? I haven't got time for you right now.

"Thank you for the offer, but I'll be fine," she responded stubbornly, drinking the last bit from her cup.

"What, you don't like help?"

"It's not that I don't like help, I know I can do it on my own. Thank you anyways. I really do have to go. Thanks for the coffee, you are now officially forgiven," she said, getting up and putting on her jacket. "It's been nice meeting you, Ryan. I'm sure we will run into each other again some time."

He got up, helped her with her jacket. As he pulled himself up, he knocked his open cup of coffee over, splashing her with what was left in the cup.

"Damn, I'm so sorry, I'm such a klutz sometimes," he said as he tried to wipe the liquid from her jacket.

Oh, my gawd! What did I do to deserve you?

"Stop, please, just stop. I know it was an accident. I just need to go. Thanks again for the coffee." She stated on the verge of anger, turning to leave.

He fished out a card from his pocket and handed it to her. "Sure. Take my card. I'm here to help whenever you need it."

Don't need that kind of help.

Without looking at it, she tucked it into her pocket. "Thanks again," she said and left the coffee shop.

Chapter 4

Emma unloaded the bags of groceries from the car, placing them on the kitchen table. Parking at the curb had caused her to make three trips to get all the bags inside and by the end of it, she was tired. She hung her coffee stained jacket over the kitchen chair, and went upstairs to see how her mom was doing.

Opening the door quietly, she saw that her mom was still sleeping and returned to the kitchen to put the items away where she thought they would go. Slipping her jacket on again with the intention of tackling the snow on the driveway, she stepped outside, and noticed the walkway had already been cleared. Moving forward, it surprised her that the driveway had been near finished as well. And there, standing at the end, cleaning up the last of it, was Ryan.

"Hey," she said as she approached him. "You didn't have to do that."

"I know, just helping out. I had it on my to-do list today."

"Well, thank you. It's appreciated. How did you know where I was? Are you stalking me?"

"And what if I was?" he paused momentarily to see her reaction which was utter surprise. "No, seriously. You said you were Susan's daughter. I normally do your mom's driveway in the wintertime. I help out where I can. I've been doing it for years. Had I known you were going to be here, it would have been done earlier."

"Thank you again. I didn't know you had that arrangement with my mom. This does save me time. I've got lots to do."

"I'm sure you do. I don't think Susan has had anyone here for a couple of weeks. How is she doing?"

"You really do know my Mom?"

"I just told you I did, she's a wonderful lady. I love the things in her store. I often pick up a few things and send them to my mom. It keeps me in her good graces when I don't visit for a while."

"Oh, so you're a kiss ass kind of guy," she laughed.

"Guilty. A clumsy kiss ass kind of guy it appears," he laughed with her looking at the stains on her jacket. His crooked smile along with the now rosy cheeks gave him a sex appeal that was hard to ignore for Emma. "I'll have that jacket cleaned for you."

Emma ran a hand across the stain. "No need. I'm sure it will wash out, but thank you for the offer. Mom's not doing so well," she admitted.

"Anything I can help with? I noticed that you didn't look at the card that I gave you. I'm a caregiver. I was doing my internship in the city as a physician, but after my wife died, I gave that up. Medicine failed me. But I love caring for people so I opened my own business here, taking care of those that need my services."

"I'm sorry. No, I didn't look at the card but I would have later. So what exactly do you offer?"

"I'll tell you what, I'm not working this weekend. If you feel you need a break or just someone to talk with while your mom is resting, come over to my place. We can talk and I'll fill you in. I can only imagine how much there is for you to do since she hasn't had help for a while."

"That does sound like a plan. Where do you live?"

He pointed to a bungalow with a large window in front and a small porch. "The one with the blue garage. You can't miss it. I'm the only one in the neighborhood with a blue garage."

She chuckled. "Why blue?"

"So that you can't miss it, why else?"

"So you invite a lot of strangers over, giving directions to the blue garage?"

He shook his head flashing that crooked smile once again. "No, the house came that way. I just haven't repainted. But see how handy that comes in?"

"Yes, it does," she replied, amused. "I'll take you up on that offer at some point. Thank you. I should get back in. I appreciate what you've done."

"No problem. Happy to help. Wish your mom a speedy recovery for me."

"I'll do that. Thank you. I think while I'm out here, I'll put the car into the driveway."

"Yes, I'm done." He scooped up two more shovels of snow, throwing it onto the pile on the side of the driveway while Emma got into her car. He watched as she backed the car up and then pulled it forward, and parked it.

"You really did save me time. Thank you, again. It's very appreciated."

"No problem. See you soon. Call me if you need help with anything." Ryan turned and walked down the sidewalk to his house.

"Will do," she called out as she went back the front door the house.

Once inside, with her jacket and boots put away, she pulled the list from her purse to see what still needed doing. It was after three o'clock, she knew she wouldn't be able to do much without waking her mom. She could do some dusting, check to see what laundry needed to be done, and fix dinner after that. She went upstairs once more, quietly checked the laundry hamper in her mom's bedroom, and as she was about to leave with it, her mom spoke up.

"Honey, what are you doing?"

"I'm just going to do some laundry for you. How are you feeling?"

"Tired. I'm always tired."

"How about we get you up for a bit, I'll change the sheets on the bed. It's always nice to get into a bed with fresh sheets. I can get you settled into the recliner in the office and you can watch a bit of TV while I make your bed."

"You don't have to go to that trouble."

"Stop, Mom. You took care of me for so many years and I know it was a thankless job. It's my turn. I'm honored to be able to take care of you now. I want to do this. No, I need to do this, so please, let me."

"All right, Emmie." She moved over to the side of the bed so that she could get up.

Emma offered her assistance then walked with her into the office. She helped her mom get comfortable in the navy blue upholstered recliner, pushing the backrest back so that her feet were lifted off the floor and placed the floral rose quilt over her to keep her warm. She turned on the TV and handed the remote to her mom. Beside the chair, there was a small love seat in the same upholstered fabric as the recliner, and a teak coffee table in front of that. To the right of her mom, a small, higher side table. The windows were covered with white sheers and cream-colored drapes that matched the carpet on the floor.

"Can I get you something to eat or drink?" Emma asked.

"A tea would be nice. The lemon ginger tea that I have in the cupboard on the right side of the sink."

"I'll get that for you right now and then I'll make your bed." Emma left her mom, went down to the kitchen, and plugged in the kettle. While the water was heating, she rummaged through the cupboard to find the tea that her mom requested and then pulled out a mug.

She returned to her mom's office with a mug of tea, milk, and sugar on a tray and placed it beside her mom. "Is there anything else I can get you? Some cookies to tie you over until dinner?"

"No, dear, I'm fine." Susan nodded as she lifted the mug with caution, her lack of strength evident.

"Let me get the sheets off your bed and put the laundry in and then I'll come sit with you."

Emma re-entered her mother's bedroom, after pulling clean sheets from the linen closet, and remade the bed. She checked the ensuite bathroom, making sure there were enough supplies and replaced the towels that she had put into the laundry earlier. She did a quick clean of the sink and toilet and when she was satisfied, she checked the main bathroom. It was mostly in a fair state except for the bathtub that looked like it required a deep clean. The mat needed to be lifted and the bath chair that her mom used called for a good cleaning as well. She made a mental note to replace the chair. Thirty minutes later, Emma stepped into the office again and her mom was fast asleep in the recliner.

Emma spent the next half hour cleaning the tub and then went to the basement to put the laundry into the dryer. Back in the kitchen, she added the bath chair to her list of things to get as well as a bell. One that could be heard downstairs if her mom needed something.

She prepared a light dinner, baked chicken breasts with steamed green beans and mashed potatoes, and when it was done, she carried two plates to the office. She placed the food on the coffee table and gently woke her mom.

"Oh, I must have dozed off again. Something smells good," Susan stated in a broken husky voice.

"I made dinner. You haven't been eating well which may be why you are feeling so tired. Let's get some strength back into you," she responded.

"I'm not sure how much I can eat, but I'll give it a try."

"I cut up your chicken for you so that you wouldn't have to fuss with that. Eat what you can. It will be better than not eating at all. Just try, you're too thin right now."

"Thank you Emma."

They watched a rerun of Friends and laughed as Ross struggled with leather pants in a date's bathroom. "I've always loved this show and could watch the reruns forever," Susan said laughing.

"Yeah, it was a great show. I think this is one of the funniest Ross moments."

When they finished dinner, Emma carried the plates to the kitchen, tidied up, and returned upstairs to help her mom into bed once more. Her mom commented on how nice it felt, with the clean sheets and thanked her daughter.

"Is there anything else I can do for you?"

"I'll be fine, dear. You go and relax. I'll call you if I need you."

"I may head over to Ryan's house. I met him today in the grocery store. He says he knows you and wishes you a speedy recovery. He shoveled the driveway. We had a good chat."

"Yes, I know Ryan. He's a sweet young man that has come to my aid many times. I've always liked him."

"If you need me, mom, your cell phone is next to you. Don't hesitate to call. Okay?"

"I will, dear. I'm tired and I'm sure I'll just sleep. You go and have some company."

Emma leaned over and kissed her mom's cheek, pulled the door almost closed so that she could hear her if she called out. She went back to the basement, and pulled the laundry into a basket, folding the items that didn't need ironing and half-folding the ones that did. A job she would tackle over the next few days, she thought. She was pleased to see that the stains that were on her jacket had come out as she had predicted.

When she was done, as tired as she was, she felt helpless, and in need of some company. She found Ryan's card, and studied it for a moment. She wondered what else she could do for her mom and thought that he might have answers for that. She called his number, feeling a little guilty that it may be too late but when he picked up after one ring, answering with a pleasant voice, she didn't feel bad anymore.

"Hi, Ryan, it's Emma. Are you busy?"

"No, just watching some TV. Why, do you need something?"

"I wanted to ask you some questions. May I come over for a few minutes?"

"Yes, come over. I'll see you in a bit." He disconnected the call.

Emma put on her boots and jacket and after locking the front door, she went to Ryan's house. As she stepped onto the porch, the door opened, and he invited her in.

"Let me take your jacket," he said, helping her out of it. "The coffee stain came out, great." He hung it on a hook by the door. She removed her snow-covered boots and followed him into the den, further back in the house. He had a fire going in the fireplace. Scented candles had been lit on the side tables at the ends of the sectional sofa, as well as on the table in front of it, giving a warm ambiance to the room and a hint of an apple pie aroma. The TV was still going, but the volume had been muted.

"What can I get you to drink?" he asked as he indicated for her to sit.

"I'd love a glass of wine if you have an open bottle." She noted the picture of a young woman on the mantle of the fireplace and assumed that she was the wife he lost.

"White or red? Both are easy."

"Then, white please."

Ryan stepped out of the room and returned moments later with two glasses of white wine. "You mentioned you had questions," he said as he handed her the drink and sat next to her.

"Yes, but before I ask, tell me more about you and your services."

"I gave up on becoming a doctor, as I told you earlier, and decided to come here for a fresh start. I noticed right away that there wasn't much help in the community for those that were ill as far as at-home medical services were concerned. I go into people's homes, help the elderly, or otherwise people that can no longer do things for themselves. If they are bedridden, I help with exercises so that their muscles remain usable. Muscle atrophy can be difficult to bounce back from. I help with bathing, meds, foot care, companionship. I also do grocery shopping or light housekeeping, anything I can do to make people's lives easier as they battle whatever ails them. They need to focus on getting better. For those that won't be getting better, I have enough medical knowledge to offer nursing support to keep them comfortable in their last days. I do have certification."

"You do this all on your own?"

"I did when I first started out, but as the business grew, I hired and trained staff to help. We are now a team of twenty, half of them are part-time. I like to have people that can dedicate themselves to the same clients until they are no longer needed."

"Wow, you must be doing well."

"It's a good business but it's hard on the heart sometimes."

"Yes, I can only imagine." She sipped her wine as she considered the emotions that his staff have to deal with.

"Tell me, what questions do you have?"

Emma hesitated for a moment. He was a stranger to her, but only because her mom said she knew him, and that he was a good man, did she decide to lay it all out. "I told you earlier that my mom has been ill." Her voice hitched as she continued on. "Today, I found out that she has stage four breast cancer." She could feel the tears burning as they formed in the corners of her eyes. She realized in that moment that she hadn't taken the time to cry it out when she found out. Now the emotion of it all came crashing down on her. She couldn't control it.

"Yes, I thought I saw something in her the last time I saw her. She looked ill. I told her to see the doctor and she promised she would. That was a while ago," he commented. He saw Emma struggle with her emotions.

"The cancer has gotten into her lungs, liver, and bones. She's been given only a few weeks to live," she cried.

Ryan moved next to her and pulled her in for a hug. At that moment, she fell apart for a good five minutes, sobbing into his shoulder. He ran a hand up and down her back to help soothe her, knowing that she needed to cry it out, as did he, when he had been in the same situation with his wife. Cancer had run through her like fire, and he'd lost her within eighteen months of diagnosis. He knew some of what she was feeling.

When Emma calmed down, she pulled from the hug feeling embarrassed. "Sorry, I didn't mean to fall apart. It's been difficult finding this out. I had no idea she had even been sick. She didn't want to worry me," she stammered, wiping at her eyes with the sleeve of her sweater.

"Hey, I know what you are going through and I'm sorry that you have to go through this."

"My Mom said she had breast cancer five years ago. She had a lumpectomy, followed by chemo and radiation. She thought she beat it. I didn't even know she had cancer back then. She hid it well. But she had my father at that time for support. Now, she's alone."

"She's not alone, she has you."

"Yes, I know. But if I had known earlier, I could have been there for her while she went through treatments. Now, I need to know everything I can do to help her. That's why I'm here." She wiped her eyes dry, with a tissue that she pulled from her jeans pocket.

"Tell you what. I have some resources in the office that I can give you. A checklist of things to do, things to watch for, tips on how to keep your mom comfortable, that kind of thing. I'll go into the office tomorrow and get you what you need. It will help to have it all in front of you, rather than me telling you. You'd forget some things for sure."

"Yes, thank you."

"And, know this. I'm here to help in whatever way I can. I'm two doors away and you can call me anytime. One thing that I think will be very important for you is this: You need to be able to step away from it from time to time for your own health. I know you love your mother and want to be there for whenever she needs you but do yourself a favor, step away when you can, like you are now while she's sleeping. But don't talk or think about it. Instead, do something you enjoy doing. What you are about to go into will be draining, both physically and mentally. It's not easy watching someone die. Especially one that is so close to your heart."

"I know, but that won't be easy either. It makes sense, I'll be stronger with the break but it's going to be so hard. I want to be with her. I don't have much time left with her."

"I'm here for you, whenever you need me. I'll help with whatever I can. And now, I'm going to send you home so that you can get yourself to bed and get some much needed sleep. I'm hoping the wine will help with that."

As she stood, he got up, too, and they walked to the front door. She slipped into her boots and jacket and turned to him once more. "Thank you again. You've been very kind."

"Emma, I care. I'm always just a call away. Count on that," he said and pulled her in for a hug.

She felt the comfort of the hug and let it last.

Oh, I could get used to this.

She let her head rest against his shoulder and felt a sense of belonging, which confused her. When she looked up at him, seeing the blue eyes studying her face, she had the urge to kiss him but instead, moved back. "Thank you, good night." She pulled the door open and stepped out.

"Good night. Get some sleep. I'll see you tomorrow." He closed the door, knowing that he was now caught up in something that may change his life.

Chapter 5

Emma rose early to do the ironing before her mother woke, and at eight o'clock, she had finished the chore and carried the laundry basket upstairs. She opened the door of her mother's room quietly and peeked in, discovering that her mom was trying to get out of bed.

"Good morning, let me help you," she said, quickly stepping into the room and setting the basket down. "Where are you going?"

"Bathroom dear. Good morning."

She helped her mom onto her feet and walked with her and once she was inside, Emma pulled the door closed and went to straighten the sheets on the bed.

Moments later, Susan reentered the bedroom and Emma suggested that she go into the office. "I'll bring up breakfast for you and it will give me a chance to vacuum and dust your room. What would you like to eat?"

"Just some tea and toast. That'll be fine."

"Mom, you need to eat more and build up your strength again."

"I'll have lunch later. I'm not hungry right now so a slice of toast is all I need." Susan assured with slight impatience.

After tucking the quilt around her mother in the recliner, she turned on the television, handed her the remote and proceeded to the kitchen to fix breakfast. She returned 15 minutes later with a tray of tea and toast and a few pieces of a honeydew melon, and a mug of coffee for herself, and sat with her mom for a while.

"Emma, we need to talk about what's to happen when I die."

No, I can't do this.

This was the conversation that Emma didn't want. She was praying all along that when she spoke to the oncologist, it won't be as bad as her mom made it out to be. It might be unrealistic, she knew, but she wasn't prepared to say goodbye to her mom yet.

"Can it wait?" Emma asked.

"Well, not really. I want to make sure you know my wishes before I die."

"Mom, I'm not ready to hear this. I'm still adjusting to the fact that you are terminally ill. Can we do this another time?"

"No Emma, please, I don't know how much time I have. So, let's get this done so that I don't have to think about it anymore." she demanded.

Realizing how selfish she was being, Emma looked at her mom with tears in her eyes, "I'm sorry, whatever you want."

Softening her tone, "Good. I want you to open the top drawer of the desk, there is a folder in there with all the information that you will need to put me to rest."

Emma retrieved an orange file folder from the drawer. She sat down beside her mom and opened it. Directly inside was an invoice from Scott's Funeral Home.

"The funeral home has been notified of my circumstances. I have picked out my coffin and paid for it, and for the services that they provide."

Emma turned the page and found an invoice from the cemetery that was marked paid.

"I've notified the people at Willowbrook Memorial Park that it won't be long and paid for the services to have me buried next to your dad. I've also paid for the etching on the headstone. If you turn the page, you'll see what I want on it."

"Why have you done all this? I would have taken care of things," Emma said, feeling as if her mother didn't think she was competent enough to do this.

"Emmie, please understand, I just wanted to make things easier for you. I know it's not easy losing a parent. I remember when I buried my father. He was all I had left because my mother had passed years before. I still miss them terribly. When your grandfather died, I was devastated and had trouble focusing on what needed to be done. I was fortunate enough to have a sister and in our grief, we just barely managed to get my father buried and his estate settled. It's too much during such an emotional time. I'm saving you from going through that, helping the process where I can so that you don't have to worry so much about all the details."

"I get that mom. It just makes me feel like you don't trust what I would do for you, but I guess that's being selfish. Just like me thinking that you should have told me about your illness from the get to, that's being selfish too, right?"

"You're not a selfish person. Never have been. As I said, I didn't want to worry you and now, this, it's to make your life easier. Now, let's move on."

Torn with emotions of sadness, anger, and sympathy, Emma turned over the page and under it was a list of companies and account numbers and contact information.

"This is a list of all the utility accounts, bank accounts, and so forth. You will need this to close accounts as you see fit. The house is paid for and it will be yours to do with as you please. You can stay in it or sell it, that's up to you. I don't want to change your life in any way. You decide. If you stay, you'll need those numbers to have the utilities put into your name. Your father and I have three bank accounts. One business, one saving, and our checking account. The money in the savings and checking accounts will be yours. The business, well, that depends on what you want done with it."

"What do you mean?" Emma asked.

"Again, you can choose to sell the business or run it yourself. It's a profitable business. I've never had a bad year. The store is on a lease, you'll find the business papers for that in separate folders in the desk. I have my usual source suppliers that treat me well. It's kept me going with some nice profits. If you chose to sell, I know that Katie Simmons would like to take it over. Something you'll have to discuss with her but be kind as she has kept the store going for the last year in my absence. A lifesaver."

"I met her yesterday. The store was busy when I stopped in there before coming here. She seems like a very nice, kind lady."

"She is and she's one of my closest friends. She calls me every day to see how I'm doing." Susan paused, taking a sip of tea. "The decision is yours, though. Do with it as you please."

"Thank you, Mom, I'll have to think about it." Emma shuffled through the papers.

"At the back, you will find the name and phone number of my lawyer. A will has been drawn up and as I said, you are the beneficiary of everything. One thing that I do ask of you, and it's not in the will, please find it in your heart to help out this community in some way. They have helped your father and I many times over the years. There are wonderful people here as you know. You met Ryan. No better man around, in my opinion. Helpful, kind, never has anything bad to say about anyone. He's always looking on the bright side of things, no matter how difficult they get. Treat him well if you decide to stay friends with him. He certainly has helped me since your dad passed."

"I'll do that, Mom. I'll find a way to help."

"Now, about my care before my death."

"You don't have to worry about that. I'm here and I'll stay for as long as you need me."

"That's my girl, I was hoping you'd say that. But again, a few things I want you to know." Susan paused a bit, sipped her tea again, and with shaky hands brought the toast to her mouth for a bite. "I'm only home now because I insisted that I didn't want to die in the hospital and that you'd be here to take care of me until the end. Please don't put me in the hospital again. I want to die here. I need to be here where I feel comfortable. When the time comes, I'd like you to call a nurse, her number is written on the front cover of the file. She will come and give me what I need to stay comfortable until I pass."

"But they may be able to help you at the hospital," Emma said desperately.

"Why, dear? Why would I want to live a little longer in discomfort or pain? My time has come and I've accepted it. You have to as well. I'm ready to be with your dad again."

Emma tried to wipe the flowing tears away, but there were too many. "I still need you," she cried, feeling like a little girl.

"Emmie, you are a grown woman and you've been taking care of yourself for years now. You don't need me. You want my love and that will always be there. Even after I'm gone, you'll feel it because your father and I will be with you. Your father and I will remain in your heart."

"I know," she said like a child. She tried desperately to regain some control as she needed to appear strong for her mother. It wasn't a time to break down. "When is your next appointment with a doctor?" she asked.

"I don't have one. I've been sent home to die and they've given me everything I need to be able to do that at home."

"Can I speak with your oncologist tomorrow?"

"There's no point. Nothing is going to change, but if you feel the need, her number is by the phone downstairs."

"I just need to hear things from her. I have questions that I need answered."

"Then you call her if it's going to help settle your mind. Now, I'm tired and would like to go back to bed."

"Give me a few minutes, Mom, I'd like to run the vacuum through there and do some dusting."

"You can leave that for a little later. I really do need to lie down now," Susan responded.

Emma saw the weariness on her mother's face. "Will it disturb you if I run the vacuum downstairs?" she asked as she helped her mother up from the chair.

"I won't hear it. You do what you need to do."

"Ryan said he was going to drop by with some information for me. Do you mind if I ask him in for a bit?"

"He'd be good company for you. I like Ryan. You might want to go to the store and talk to Katie. Help her out if you can. She's been doing it on her own for a long time now. I can't get in there anymore to help. I'm sure she would appreciate the help. Tell her I say hello and a big thank you for all she's done."

Emma tucked her mother back into bed, carried the tray of dishes to the kitchen, and cleaned up. She then ran the vacuum through the first floor of the house and did the dusting afterward. She took a quick look around and felt satisfied.

Feeling cleaner already.

She checked her watch, noting it was after eleven o'clock and decided to run over to the store to talk with Katie.

The shop was busy again, and she felt badly that Katie had to deal with it all by herself. When she approached the counter, she asked Katie if she could help with anything.

"Why don't you stay here with me for a bit, watch how I ring in the sales, and then you can take that over for a bit."

Emma stood behind the counter, watched Katie, and helped wrap the items that had been sold. Katie greeted customers by name and introduced them to Emma, noting that she was Susan's daughter. Everyone seemed pleased to finally meet the girl Susan always spoke about with such pride.

It was after two when Emma checked her watch again. "I have to go home and get some food into Mom. I didn't realize how much time had gone by. Do you mind if I leave? I'll be back tomorrow and we can work out a schedule so that I can be here to help and give you a break as I become more familiar with things."

"That's fine, you go take care of your mom. I'm glad you are here for her. As for the store, I'm okay doing this on my own. But anytime you want to stop in and help, that would be welcome as well."

"Thank you, Katie. I'll see you tomorrow," Emma replied, grabbing her jacket.

When she arrived home, she went upstairs to check on her mom and was horrified to discover her on the floor.

"Mom, are you okay?" she asked, rushing to her in a panic.

"I'm fine. I tried getting out of bed to go to the bathroom and my legs just gave out on me I guess. Help me, please."

Emma waited until her mom was done and helped her back into bed.

"How long were you lying on the floor?"

"Not long,"

"You should have called me."

"I couldn't reach my phone."

"I'm going to do something about that. I don't ever want you to go through that again." Emma fussed with the blankets a bit. "Can I get you something to eat?"

"Not right now, Emmie. I think I'd like some soup and a sandwich for dinner if you don't mind fixing that for me later."

"I'll be happy to fix you anything you want," Emma responded.

"I'm tired now, I'd like to sleep. You can tell me later what you've been up to."

"Sure. Mom, please use the phone to call me if you need anything. Don't try to get out of bed on your own. I'm here to help." She got up and left her mother's bedroom, leaving the door slightly ajar.

When she returned downstairs, she called Ryan and told him what had occurred. He advised that a walker could help Susan get up and move to the bathroom if she was feeling weak.

"I'll get you one on loan tomorrow," Ryan said. "See how that works. If she needs more, I might be able to find a smaller style wheelchair that she can use to get from one room to another upstairs if she needs to."

"Thank you, Ryan," she replied. "I think I should get help in here. Someone that can be here for her while I'm out. I need to help Katie with the store. It's so busy and she has no one to help her. I just need someone to be here in case mom wakes up and needs help. She sleeps a lot."

"I can help with that. I know of a few women in the community, people that Susan knows, who might be willing to sit there for a while when you are busy with shopping or in the store. I'll ask around."

"You are a lifesaver, Ryan, thank you."

"I'm busy right now but can I drop by with the papers that I said I'd get you? After dinner perhaps?"

"Yes, of course. I'll see you then." She disconnected the call and went upstairs to retrieve her laptop from her bedroom.

Emma sat in the family room, researching what to anticipate when someone dies. She determined that death has a pre-active phase that can last two to three weeks and an active phase that lasts around three days. She noticed the same signs in her mother as she studied the indicators of the pre-active period. She continued reading through the active phase to know what to anticipate.

Tears rolled down her face as she read. Her heart aching with the knowledge of what was to come, but she knew she needed to remain strong for her mom. She closed the laptop and realized that Christmas was only two weeks away. She wondered if her mom would survive that long.

There was nothing in the house to make it look holiday festive. It was going to be a big task, but she decided to dress the house for her mom. Her mom always loved Christmas, and she was sure that this would help her mom's spirits. She wanted this to be the best last Christmas that her mom would know.

Emma went to the basement, hunting for decorations that her mom had collected over the years. She found 4 large boxes and two small bins of things she needed. She was careful as she carried them up the stairs and placed them in the living room. While searching for the Christmas decorations, she came across a few items that would be of help now with her mom. A large tray that looked big enough to extend past the arms of the recliner in the office, a newer tub chair than the one currently used, and a four-point cane. She took those items upstairs as well and cleaned each piece for use.

She quietly started to rearrange the living room furniture so that she could put up the artificial tree that her mom loved. She pulled the pieces from the box and built it from the base up, standing it in the corner of the room by the sliding glass patio doors. She added the lights, ornaments, ribbon, and tinsel to the tree and felt proud of her accomplishment when she was done.

In the kitchen, she heated a can of soup and prepared a sandwich for her mom, then carried the tray upstairs, placing it on the table in the office. She went to her mom's room to wake her. With only a gentle nudge, her mother was awake.

"What time is it?" she asked.

"It's after five. You need to eat something," Emma responded. "I'll help you up and you can sit in the office. Your soup is waiting for you."

"Thank you Emmie. I'll be there in a minute. Just help me up and I'll be fine."

"Wait here for a second. I have something for you. I forgot to bring it up earlier." Emma raced down the stairs, retrieved the cane, and raced back to her mother's room.

"I found this in the basement. I thought it would be good for you to use. It will help you out of bed and give you extra support when walking."

Susan looked at the cane, remembering the last time it was used. "That's what your father used in his last weeks. It did help him as I'm sure it will help me. Thank you. I forgot I had this."

She waited for her mom to come out from the bathroom and walked with her to the office. Susan sat in the recliner and Emma placed the large tray across the arms of the recliner then placed the soup and sandwich on the tray. Her mom ate as Emma told her of her day.

It was after six when Susan said she'd like to go back to bed and do some reading. Emma placed cushions behind her mom to help prop her up. She turned on the table lamp which was bright enough to allow her to read.

"Ryan said he was going to drop by with something later. If you need me, call me. That's what I'm here for. Okay?"

"You go enjoy the company. I'll be fine."

"I'll come up and check on you later."

At six-forty five, the doorbell rang. Emma turned on the hall light and opened the door. Ryan stood there with a large bag in one hand and a folder in the other. Snow covered his head and shoulders from what must have dropped from the small roof over the front door.

"Have you had dinner yet?" he asked with a big, crooked smile, holding up the bag.

"No. I made some soup and a sandwich for my mom at five, but I wasn't hungry then. I was about to fix something."

"No need to do that, I've brought dinner for the two of us."

"Come in, please, you're letting the cold in," she laughed. "What happened to you?"

"It's a timing thing, I guess. Somehow, these crazy things just happen to me. I approached the door and bam, the snow dropped on me from the roof."

"Mishaps seem to be your thing," she laughed. "Come in."

He handed her the bag and folder, then brushed the excess snow from his head and shoulders before entering. He removed his boots and jacket, hanging the jacket on the hook by the door. "The folder contains the papers that I said I would get for you but before we get into that, let's eat. I'm hungry."

She led him into the kitchen and retrieved two dinner plates. "What are we having?"

"Ah, this is something special. I have a friend who owns a restaurant in town. I brought lasagna, garlic bread, and a side salad."

"Ooh. Sounds delightful," Emma responded, opening the bag. Her appetite built as she took in the aroma of the food. She pulled out the contents of the bag, placed them on the table, and got the cutlery they would need for the meal. The lasagna and garlic bread had been keeping warm in the foil containers that they came in.

"Here," she said, handing him a spatula, "you dish it up, I'll get drinks. What would you like?" she asked.

"Shoot, that's what I forgot. You dish up, I've got a bottle of wine sitting on my porch. I had to put it down to lock the door. Be right back," he said, heading to the front entrance. He stepped into his boots, and without putting his jacket on, he was out the door, only to return moments later with the wine bottle in hand.

"You shouldn't go out without a jacket. It's too cold for that," Emma scolded.

"Yes, Mom," he feigned. "For the minute I was out there, there's no chance of me getting sick."

She smiled at him, admiring the grin he flashed. She retrieved wine glasses and a corkscrew which she handed him. He opened the wine and filled the both glasses.

"Dig in," he said. "Don't let it get cold."

"You're spoiling me," she replied. "Thank you." She took a bite of the lasagna. "Wow, this is fantastic," she said with a mouthful of food.

"Yes, he's an excellent chef. Why do you think we are friends?" he said, making her laugh.

"I see, you're the kind of man that only makes friends with people that you can gain something from?"

"Well, there is that," he paused, "but no. He and I have been friends since I moved here. We go fishing in the summer. It's a great way to relax."

"I'm sure." She sipped her wine. They ate while chatting about hobbies and interests, getting to know one another better.

"How's your mom doing?" he asked, as he took his last bite of dinner. He didn't want to bring up that conversation through the meal as she deserved to get her thoughts away from that for a bit.

"I left her reading, but I guarantee you that if I went upstairs right now, she'd be fast asleep. That's all she's up to doing these days. She sleeps all the time and only gets up to eat and to use the bathroom."

"Her body is fighting cancer and that's tiring. And if it's in her lungs and liver and bones, that's a huge fight she knows she won't win."

Emma sat silently. She was glad she had almost finished her dinner as now her appetite was gone. It wasn't easy to think about her mom dying. "I wish I knew what to do to help her be as comfortable as possible."

"I've got some stuff in the folder for you to read. It will help."

"I've done some research as to what to expect over the next few weeks, the changes that will happen in the pre-active phase and the active phase. I think that helped, too. I can watch for signs."

Ryan drank from his wine glass. "What you are about to go through over the next while, won't be easy. It's going to be hard, very hard," he stressed. "And I want you to know that I'm here to help you with whatever you need."

"Are you done?" she asked, reaching for his plate, hoping to change the subject.

"Yes, let me help clean up," he said, getting up and taking both their plates to the counter before she could. He then retrieved the containers that had leftovers in them and placed them on the counter as well.

Emma ran water and washed the plates and cutlery, placing them in the rack to dry. She then covered the container with foil and put them back into the bag.

"What are you doing?" he asked.

"Sending leftovers home with you."

He turned her so that she was facing him. "You're really sweet to do that, but I want you to have it or you can give some to your mom. You are trying to make your mom more comfortable, I'm trying to make your life a little easier."

Emma looked at him, watched as his blue eyes scanned over her face. Waited for what she hoped would come. She closed her eyes and imagined his lips brushing over hers lightly as if to ask permission.

Kiss me!

He watched as her eyes closed in expectation of a kiss and as much as he was drawn to give her exactly what she wanted, he battled with his own struggles. He couldn't help but feel like that he would be taking advantage of someone vulnerable. She was hurting and not thinking clearly. But her full lips seemed to cry out "kiss me" and he swore that one day, he'd get his fill. He needed to deal with some issues first.

When nothing happened, her eyes fluttered open, feeling foolish for allowing her imagination to take over.

Damn, stop making a fool of yourself.

Embarrassed, she stepped back and turned to the sink, took the cloth, and wiped down the counter.

"Why don't we go over the paperwork that I brought for you," he continued, noticing the embarrassment. "I'm sure there is information in that folder that will help you."

Needing to collect herself some, she responded, "Sure, why don't you go into the family room. You can light the fire and we can talk about things. I'm just going to run upstairs and check on mom."

"Sounds good." He picked up the folder from the kitchen table and went in search of the family room.

Emma ran up the stairs and pushed open the door to her mom's room. Her mom was fast asleep. She moved the book that her mom was holding to the night table, and removed the pillows that propped her up, which woke her. She helped her scoot lower under the covers and tucked the covers around her. She kissed her mom good night, turned off the light, and left the room, leaving the door slightly ajar.

She went into the main bathroom, checked herself.

Don't you look like a prize. She cleaned up the mascara that had run a little with the tears she had lost control of earlier, and then returned to the family room.

"Oh, you do know how to light a good fire," she commented, admiring the dancing flames in the open fireplace. "I don't even know what to do to light one."

"It's really quite easy, actually."

There's that irresistible smile again. She sat next to him on the sofa, and they went through the papers one by one, discussing each page. When they were done, he got up and stated that it was time for him to head home as tomorrow was a workday.

"Be sure to call me with any questions or if you need any help. And I'll call you if I find someone that can sit with your mom for a bit when you need to be out."

"Perfect. Thank you very much for everything Dinner was delicious and the information you've provided is appreciated." She walked him to the door where he put on his boots and jacket and smiled at her.

"Any time."

"Good night." She smiled as he opened the door, stepped out, wished her a good night, and was on his way. The cold blasted into the house for those few moments that the door was open. Closing it quickly, she locked it, and went back into the family room.

She took a few sips of the wine that was left in the glass and realized that she didn't know what to do to douse the fire.

What now? Can't call him. He'll think I'm stupid. Come on now, can't be that hard. She looked around the fire place to see if there were any clue's. *Maybe I should wake Mom. No, don't do that.* She contemplated the situation a moment longer. *I guess I have to call him.*

"Hi, miss me already?" he laughed, answering his phone.

"I feel stupid. I've never owned a fireplace before. What do I do use to put out the the fire? Do I just let it burn out?"

He laughed out loud. "Well, sweetie, that will take a long time."

What the hell? Why are you laughing?

"Sorry, I didn't mean to laugh. It's a gas fireplace. Just flip the switch at the right side of it. It looks like a light switch."

She looked to the right of the fireplace, and now felt totally embarrassed once again. "Got it. Thanks. Sorry to have bothered you," she stated coldly.

"Hey, no bother at all. Anytime," he chuckled.

"Good night." She disconnected the call without waiting for a reply, feeling foolish, again.

She didn't turn off the fireplace yet, instead, she drank another glass of wine, went through the papers once more, sat back, and thought about the day, Ryan, and what was still to come.

Chapter 6

Emma utilized the morning making the necessary phone calls, speaking first to her boss to let him know that she was taking a leave of absence to care for her mother, explaining what had happened.

"I'm sorry to hear about your mom. You take all the time you need. We will survive. What's important is that you don't worry about what's going on here so that you can focus on caring for your mom," Mr. Evans said.

"I may be away for at least six weeks, if not more," she told him.

"Emma, please don't worry about that. You have enough going on in your life right now. The job will be here for you when you get back."

"I'd like to set up remotely in case Nisha needs me. I'll call her next to let her know what needs to be done."

"That's fine. I will speak to IT to give authorization to get you set up, but you have to promise that it's only in case Nisha needs help and at that, only at your convenience."

"Thank you, Mr. Evans. I'll call Nisha now. Have a good day." Emma disconnected and then punched Nisha's number.

"Hey, girl! Where are you? Did you do too much partying on the weekend?"

"Good morning, Nisha. I won't be in for a while. About six weeks." As Emma explained what was happening, she couldn't control the quivering of her voice.

"I'm so sorry, Emma. If there's anything I can do, please let me know. I'll do whatever you need."

"Thank you, there's not much anyone can do. I'm trying to make her last days as comfortable as possible. You call me if you need help with anything, okay? Mr. Evans is setting me up remotely in case you require assistance with something. I'll check in with you in a couple of days."

Emma then placed a call to her mother's oncologist's office, asking for a call back from the doctor to ask a few questions. Her phone rang about an hour later.

"Thank you for returning my call so quickly," Emma said into the phone.

"How can I help you, Miss Jones?" The doctor asked.

"I'm actually embarrassed to say that I just found out on Saturday that my mom has terminal cancer. She never even mentioned that she was sick. She said she didn't want to worry me and now, I only have a few weeks with her. Can you tell me exactly what's going on?"

"It seems your mom has duped both of us. She told me that you were aware and at home taking care of her all this time. That was back in January when the cancer reoccurred." The doctor paused for a moment. "The specifics don't matter at this point, but I can tell you that we have done everything possible to get the cancer under control. Unfortunately, it's spreading faster this time and she did wait a little too long before coming to see me. I'm not sure if it would have mattered much but we might have had better control of how quickly it invaded her body. She's had all the rounds of chemotherapy and radiation that we can safely give. It's just too far gone, I'm sorry."

"So you can't do anything more for her?"

"I'm afraid not. She was in the hospital a week ago. I wondered why you hadn't visited with her. She told me that you were away on a business trip. She asked to go home to die. Said you would be there to take care of her. That's the only reason why we let her go home. Most like to spend their last days with family around them. She was going into the pre-active shut down phase. I can put you in touch with some excellent home care services if you like."

"No, thank you. That won't be necessary. A neighbor two doors down, a friend, is a home caregiver. We will be using his services. How long do you think she has?"

"I told her before she left that she needed to get her things in order. We saw signs of the body already starting to shut down."

"She sleeps a lot now," Emma said with tears streaming down her face with emotions strong and painful.

"Yes, her body is still trying to fight it, making her weak. I suspect that she will go through the active shut down process soon. I'm sorry that you have just found out. I'm sure you would have liked to be there for her through all of this. I can't imagine finding out like you did, at this stage of it. It must be very difficult for you."

"Is she in pain? She doesn't show it if she is."

"She has medication if she is in pain but I don't suspect that there would be much. She will go through changes, such as a loss of appetite, drowsiness, fatigue, her skin will get pale, she will become confused, her breathing will become labored and her kidneys will fail. Sometimes the extremities will change color. Feet and hands, they may also swell. This is how it will progress and I'm only telling you this so that you can prepare yourself."

"Yes, I have done some research and have learned about the process. Well, I guess that answers my questions. Thank you again for calling back so quickly. It's appreciated."

"You call anytime if you have more questions. Hug your mom for me."

"Will do." Emma disconnected the call and through blurred vision from the tears, she stared at her phone that she placed on the table.

More real now. How am I going to get through this?

It was nearing noon by the time Emma finished her calls and she rubbed the palms of her hands over her face, hoping to revitalize herself. Fatigue was beginning to set in. She had gotten her mother up earlier in the morning, and into the tub to bathe using the bath chair that she discovered in the basement. She let her mom wash herself, not wanting to embarrass her, then helped her out, gave her a fresh nightie to put on, and got her comfortable in the office recliner for her breakfast. Within minutes of finishing her breakfast, Susan wanted to be back in bed as the bath had taken the energy right out of her.

Now, as she sat at the kitchen table, Emma wept quietly. It was only day three, and she could feel the effects of the strain, physically and emotionally. But she knew she needed to continue as her mom would be up any time now for lunch. She gave herself a moment, putting her head on her arms on the kitchen table, and closed her eyes. She just needed a moment, she thought.

When she heard her mom moving around upstairs, she went to check on her.

"Mom, are you okay?"

"I'm so embarrassed. I couldn't help it."

"Help what, Mom."

"I'm afraid I messed my bed. I couldn't get up fast enough."

"That's okay. Let me help you to the bathroom. I'll get you a fresh nightie and a washcloth. Are you okay to wash yourself or would you like help?"

"I'll be fine."

"Alright, freshen up, put on the nightie, and I'll change your sheets in the meantime."

"Oh, Emmie, what would I do without you? You're so good to me."

"Mom, you never spanked me for wetting the bed. Did you expect that I'd be upset with you? It happens. Don't worry about it."

Using the cane, Susan walked to her bathroom. Emma followed with a fresh nightgown and a washcloth.

Emma removed the linens from the bed, and was happy to see a mattress protector under the fitted sheet. She washed and dried the area, put on fresh sheets, and fixed the blankets on top. She carried the soiled linens to the laundry basket. Her mom came out of the bathroom and handed the damp nightie to Emma who added that into the laundry basket as well.

"Did you want some lunch, Mom?" she asked.

"I'm really not hungry. The scrambled eggs that you made me this morning still have me full."

"Would you like to sit up for a while?"

"I think I'd just like to lie down. I'll read a bit," she replied.

Emma helped her to bed once more, tucked the blankets around her, and gave her the book she was reading. The title caught her attention this time. Crossing Over was not something that her mother would normally read. She was usually more into women's literature or romance novels. This was a surprise.

"Are you sure you don't want something to eat?"

"Yes, thank you, Emma. I'll have some tea, though, if you wouldn't mind making some for me."

"You only have to ask. I'll get you whatever you want."

Emma grabbed the towels from the bathrooms, put them in the laundry basket, and took the laundry down, placing the load into the washer. She went back to the kitchen, fixed her mother some tea, and took it up to her mom. As she entered the room, she saw that her mom was sleeping. She left her with a book in hand, tea on the nightstand, and went back downstairs.

She called Ryan.

"Hey, how are you? Is this a bad time to call?"

"Hi, not at all. I'm always happy to hear from you," he responded.

"Were you able to find someone to sit in with my mom from time to time?"

"Actually, yes. I was going to call you later. Is everything okay?"

"I need to pick up a couple of things but after leaving her alone the last time, I don't want to risk that again."

"I'd be happy to get what you need, send me a list."

Emma hesitated for a moment. "No, but thanks. It's personal."

"Personal for you or your mom?" he asked.

Geez, leave it alone.

"Mom."

"Let me guess. She's wetting the bed and you'd like to pick up some Depends for her."

"How did you know?" she asked in amazement.

"You forget my background. I know what happens, what's going to happen. You can ask me anything. I'll pick up a package for her. How much do you think she weighs right now?"

"I'd say about a hundred and ten pounds. She's lost so much weight."

"Small is what she will need. Is there anything else I can get? Do you need anything?"

"I'm fine. Thank you, Ryan."

"How is your day going otherwise?" he asked.

"I'm tired. It's not easy and I have a new appreciation for those who do this as a profession."

"Yes, it can be an exhausting job but it would be, more so, for you because you also have the emotional involvement. It's your mom, you want the best for her. When you do it as a profession, as much as you care for the individual, you care for many and learn to block that emotional involvement. That doesn't mean we care less or they get second-rate care, it just means we can go home at the end of the day and sleep, knowing we did the best we knew how. You toss and turn, wondering what more you can do. As a result, you get less sleep and your emotions run higher."

"I get that. It makes sense."

"You will need help, Emma. Take time for yourself so that you can step away and re-energize. It's important."

"I know, but to tell you the truth, it's only day three and I'm feeling a bit like a failure already."

"Why? What makes you feel that way?"

"I don't know, maybe because I can't make her better," she half laughed but could feel the tears forming in her eyes.

"Emma, she's not going to get better. No matter what you do. All you can do is make her comfortable. Give her what she asks for because right now, she knows best what she needs. Make sure she eats and drinks and that's about all you can do.

Keep her company when she's awake, I'm sure she'd like to spend her last days with you."

"That's the hard part. I can't sit with her without crying."

"She knows how difficult this is for you. Cry if you need to. She'll understand."

"Thank you. I needed that. I'm sorry if I disturbed you. I should get back to work."

"You didn't disturb me, I'm always here if you need to talk. What are you working on now?"

"I'm heading outside to see if I can find the Christmas lights. I'll get those up. It looks like this is the only house without decorations on the street."

"That doesn't matter. What matters is your mom."

"She's sleeping. I'll do it now while I can. I'm hoping she's still with me for Christmas. I've decorated the house a bit for her."

"You be careful. Don't go falling off any ladders."

"I won't. Thanks again, Ryan."

"No problem. Talk with you soon."

Emma pushed the end call button, put on her jacket and boots, and pressed the remote button to open the garage door in hopes that it would give her sufficient light to find the Christmas lights. She entered by way of the side door and rummaged through the garage for a half-hour before deciding to give up, having found nothing. As the garage door was closing, she spotted the box marked 'Christmas Lights' on a shelf above it. She pulled the stepladder down from its hooks, placed it under the box, and climbed up to retrieve it. She gave the box a tug to pull it down, and realized how heavy it was.

Careful, don't fall down the ladder. What use would you be then?

"What are you doing?" a voice cried out from behind her. The unexpected sound startled her, and she released hold of the box and slipped off the ladder as she turned to see who was there.

Strong arms caught her, and she found herself looking into Ryan's eyes. "I'm sorry, I didn't mean to startle you. Are you all right?"

"Yes, I'm fine, thank you. You can put me down now." she stated with irritation.

"Hmmm, I kind of like this," he said with a laugh. He noted that she wasn't amused, and set her down.

"What are you doing here? You scared the crap out of me."

"Thought I'd give you a hand. I'm the boss, and I can leave whenever I want to from work," he responded. "I picked up what you wanted me to get," he said, pointing to the bag that he had dropped, to catch her.

"Thank you. What do I owe you?" she asked.

"Dinner." He responded with that crooked smile that melted her heart whenever he used it.

"I was about to pull down that box of lights. It's heavy. If you wouldn't mind getting it down for me, I'll continue from there."

Ryan climbed the ladder, pulled the large box from the shelf, and brought it down. "Why don't you put that bag inside and I'll take the ladder out front. Then you can tell me how you want the lights put up."

"I'm fine, I can manage on my own." *Please, just go.*

"What, again you don't want help?"

Ugh. "Alright, have it your way, I'm too tired to argue. I'd like to test them first to make sure that they are all working. If they are, then we just string the lights, going from one side of the garage around to the front entrance. I think that's how Mom and Dad had it over the years."

Ryan spent the next hour, up and down on the ladder, securing the colorful lights from the eaves-trough around the front of the house. Emma had taken the bag inside, checked on her mom who still slept peacefully, and then went out to secure the large red bows to the light fixtures on both sides of the garage door. When they were finished, Emma plugged in the lights and stood back to admire the welcoming of Christmas. She took a picture with her phone and in her excitement, she hugged Ryan. "Thank you. You don't know how much this means to me. Thank you for your help," she said.

"Happy to help. So, what's for dinner?" he laughed.

"It's only two-thirty," she laughed with him. "I'll figure it out."

"Okay, you go in, do what you need to do, and be ready to go out about seven."

"What are you talking about?"

"We will be going out for dinner. I have arranged for Mrs. Conners to come over for a few hours to be with your mom while we go out. She lives just down the street and she and your mom are friends. You can check with your mom if she'd be okay with that but I'm sure it will be fine. If not, call me." He gave her a quick hug and walked to his SUV that was parked at the curb. "Seven. Be ready," he called out.

She watched in disbelief, not understanding how that came about, as he climbed into his SUV and left. She was sure she was to be cooking dinner for him as repayment.

Well that bag of Depends just got expensive.

When his vehicle drove out of sight, she went back inside, and checked on her mom, finding her awake.

"Hi, did you have a good nap?"

"It's all I can do these days. What have you been up to?"

"Ryan helped me put up the Christmas lights outside. It looks wonderful. Just like you and Dad used to do."

"That's good, dear. I wish I could see them." Emma pulled out her phone and showed her the picture she had taken.

"Oh, they look wonderful. You did a good job."

"Do you know a Mrs. Conners?"

"Yes, a dear friend that lives just down the street. She's called me a few times recently, wanting to visit with me. I just haven't been up to it."

"Ryan called her and asked if she would sit here with you. He wanted to take me out for dinner. How do you feel about that?"

"I don't know if I'll be able to stay awake to chat with her, but I'll try."

"Mom, you don't have to stay awake. She will be here to make sure that you have what you need while I'm gone. I don't want you to be alone anymore. The last time I did that, you ended up on the floor, remember? I'm not taking any more chances."

"Well, that's fine. You go and enjoy yourself with Ryan. He's a good man."

"Tell me about Mrs. Conners. How did you meet?"

Emma pulled the cushioned chair closer to the bed, and chatted with her mother. She realized that she didn't know nearly enough about her mom, her mom's friends, her life in Willowbrook. There were a lot of questions and they talked until Susan got tired again. "You nap and I'll bring up dinner for you at five. Do you have a preference?"

"I'm not hungry these days. Just some soup and crackers are good enough for me. Don't go to any bother."

"It's not a bother. I have some chicken breasts thawing. I could make that with a bit of rice and a vegetable. How does that sound?"

"Sounds like too much for me. Keep the chicken in the fridge and let's have that tomorrow when you are home for dinner. I promise I'll try to eat it then."

"Alright, I'll be back a little later with your dinner. You close your eyes. If you need anything, call me."

Emma returned the chair to its usual spot, and before she stepped out the door, she glanced back, and saw her mom was already fast asleep. She went into her own bedroom, looking for something to wear for dinner. She arrived with just a few changes of clothing as she didn't expect to be staying any length of time.

I should cancel. She felt frustrated as she fished through her bag knowing there was nothing appropriate to wear. She went to the closet, wondering if there would be something in there and was surprised to see some of her mother's clothes hanging from hangers. As she rummaged through the items, she found a white silk blouse and a pair of black slacks that looked to be her size. She knew that they were now too big for her mom because of the weight loss and decided to try them on. She was pleased with the way the clothes fit, as she checked herself in the full-length mirror.

You always had good taste mom.

After removing the clothes and placing them on the hangers again and back into the closet, she skimmed through the rest of the clothes and knew, that in a pinch, there would be other things that could be worn.

Wish I had my own clothes. I should go back and get some.

She decided that a drive back to the city to pack more things for her stay with her mom would be in order. She'd ask if Mrs. Conners would spend Saturday with her mom while she made the trip.

By 4:30 p.m., Emma showered and dried her hair before switching the laundry from the washer to the dryer. She prepared soup and crackers, as her mother requested, but also cut up an apple, thinking it may taste good, too. Stopping by the office, she placed the tray on the table and went to her mother's room.

Susan walked out of the bathroom and saw Emma waiting for her. "Emma," Susan said as she came back into the bedroom. "I'm feeling so much better."

"I'm happy to hear that. Let's get some food into you." Emma led her mom to the office where the tray awaited.

Once her mom was in the recliner with a blanket tucked around her and the extended tray placed in front of her with the food, Emma sat next to her.

"I have to run into the city at some point and pack some more clothes. I didn't know I was going to be staying longer than the weekend. Is there someone I can call to stay with you while I go?"

"Julie might be willing to stay. I'll ask her when she comes over today."

"Julie? You mean Mrs. Conners?"

"Yes, Julie Conners. She's living on her own right now. Her husband passed away about ten years ago. I'm sure she will be fine with staying. We'll ask later."

"Mom, if you could wish for anything in the world, what would it be?"

"To be with your father. I miss him terribly."

"I miss Daddy, too. You have to promise me that when you meet up with him, you'll give him a big hug and a kiss from me."

"Oh, I'll be doing my own hugging and kissing for a while. You'll just have to wait your turn," she laughed.

They watched a sitcom while Susan ate her soup, both laughing at the antics of the characters, and when it was done, they chatted a bit more about things that had been going on in Emma's life. Her mother looked disappointed when she told her that there was no man in her life and that she was all right with that.

"You need someone in your life, sweetie. A man's love, if it's true love, will be one of the best things that life can offer… and until you have that, you wouldn't know what I mean. A child's love follows and with that, it fills your heart with happiness that can't be described. You'll have to experience that also. And where would I be right now if it weren't for the love of my beautiful daughter? I'm so thankful for you and that God gifted you to me."

"Awe, you're going to make me cry again. I love you, Mom."

"Love you, too, baby girl. Now, please help me get back into bed."

"I hope you don't mind but I have nothing to wear to dinner tonight except for my jeans and sweaters that I brought. I don't know where Ryan is taking me. I saw a few things in the closet in the guest room, do you mind if I wear the black slacks and a white blouse? I tried them on and they fit."

"Wear whatever you want. I won't be needing those clothes anymore. Take what you want."

Emma pulled the blankets over her mom and gave her a kiss on the cheek. "I'm going to get dressed, is there anything you need?"

"I'm fine, dear. You go do what you need to do."

"I'll be back in a bit." Emma left to get dressed. When she was ready, she carried the tray downstairs, cleaned up the dishes, and then folded the sheets and towels that were in the dryer.

The doorbell rang while she was busy in the laundry room, and she hurried to answer the door. When she pulled the door open, a tall slender woman in her mid-fifties stood before her with a huge grin on her face.

"You must be Emma," she said with a smile as she breezed into the house. "I'm Julie Conners."

"Nice to meet you, Mrs. Conners." She extended her hand.

Instead of taking it, Julie gave Emma a quick hug. "I've heard so much about you. It's so nice to finally meet you. And please, call me Julie."

"May I take your coat, Julie?"

Julie slipped out of it and hung it on a hook beside the door. "This will do just fine. Now, where's your mom? I've truly missed her so much."

The green sweater Julie wore over a beige blouse brought out the green in her eyes which gleamed with anticipation. She wore brown slacks and slipped on a pair of gold slippers that she pulled from her purse. Her hair was blondish with greying strands, short and in loose curls that helped hide the thinning of her hair. She wore little makeup on her face that was lightly defined with wisdom lines.

"She's upstairs. She's not very strong anymore and sleeps a lot. She's a little worried that she may drop off to sleep during your conversations," Emma commented. "I assured her that it would be all right. That you wouldn't mind."

"I don't mind that a bit. I'll keep her company while she's awake and keep her safe while she's asleep. I'm so glad that Ryan asked me."

"Let me take you up," Emma replied, leading the way up the stairs. When they got to the top of the stairs, Emma peeked in and saw that her mom was still awake, reading.

"Mom? Julie Conners is here."

"Oh, show her in please." she replied cheerfully.

Julie strode into the room, going right over to her friend. She sat on the bed and gathered Susan into a heartfelt hug. "I've missed you dearly."

"I've missed you, too. Please, sit and make yourself comfortable. We have things to talk about."

Julie sat in the chair that Emma had placed beside the bed earlier, putting her purse on the floor.

"Before Emma leaves, we need to ask you for another favor."

"Anything for you Susan. You know that."

"Emma needs to run into the city to pack more of her things. I'm afraid I didn't prepare her for the need for her to stay here for a time. Would you be willing to stay with me while she's gone? She's afraid to leave me alone now."

"Absolutely. Just say when, Emma, and I'll be happy to take care of your mom for you," she said, looking at Emma.

"Thank you so much, Mrs. Conners. I appreciate it. I'll let you know when I plan to go," Emma replied.

"It's Julie," she reminded. "I'm ready on a moment's notice. Now, you go. I'm sure Ryan will be here momentarily."

Emma felt dismissed but didn't care. She knew that her mom would enjoy spending time with her friend.

As she reached the bottom of the stairs, the doorbell rang once more, and she opened the door to the handsome Ryan with his crooked smile.

"Hi," she said. "Come in while I get my purse and jacket."

"You look very pretty," he commented. "It wasn't until I got home that I realized I had put you in an awkward position. So dinner plans were dependent on what you were wearing. I know you came here with only a few things because you had only planned on staying the weekend."

"Yes, that's true, but Mom has a closet full of clothes she's not wearing anymore," she laughed. "I'm going to head back home and pack more things that will last me for the next few weeks."

"Let's talk about that over dinner." Ryan helped her with her jacket. She retrieved her purse from the kitchen, then slipped into her boots, and they were on their way.

Chapter 7

"Well, since you're all dolled up, I'll take you to my friends' restaurant. I'm sure he'd be happy to have us." Ryan opened the door and helped her into the SUV. "I wasn't sure what you'd be wearing and he does have a dress code. So it was either the diner on the corner of Main and Fifth for a pizza or burger, or Giovanni's House." He closed the door and got into the driver's side.

"This isn't dolled up but it's not jeans," she laughed. "As I said, I really didn't have much of a choice. I'm anxious to get home and get some things."

"Where in the city do you live?"

"I'm on the northern end of the city actually. York Mills and Bayview area. Close enough to downtown to take advantage of what the city has to offer and far enough away that I feel safe in my home."

"I understand that. I lived right in the heart of things. Had a condo that overlooked the lake. It was beautiful, but when you listen to the news about the break-ins and the stabbings and so forth, I'm glad I'm not there anymore. It doesn't get better, only worse. I know crime is everywhere these days, but there's just less of it in smaller communities."

The ten-minute ride took them to an older Victorian-style home. Emma wasn't sure why he had stopped there. Ryan got out of the SUV came round to her side and helped her out.

"Why are we stopping here? I thought you said we were going to a restaurant."

"This is it. It's a legit restaurant, don't worry. My friend, Lorenzo, bought this house and converted it into a very profitable restaurant. You'll love this. Come," he said, taking her hand and leading the way.

As she approached, it felt like a home instead of a restaurant. She saw a wide pathway that led between the houses to a parking lot at the back. Ryan opened the door without knocking and stepped in. The front entrance was grand. A bench seat along one wall, a coat check on the other. A petite young lady, dressed in a streamlined black dress with a white silk print scarf and white belt, stood behind a small counter. She immediately looked up from what she was doing and smiled with a perky greeting as she pushed her golden curls off her shoulder.

"Good evening. Welcome to Giovanni's House. Do you have reservations?"

"Hi there," Ryan spoke up. "No, we don't, but tell Lorenzo that Ryan is here to see him. He'll know."

"Very well, I'll be back in a moment." While they waited, they removed their jackets and handed them to a young man at the coat check.

Before the young lady returned to her station, a voice bellowed from the top of the stairs. "Ryan. How good to see you!"

Emma looked up the spiral staircase and saw a middle-aged man, who carried a few pounds too many, work his way down the stairs. His black and gray hair, thinning on top, and a mustache of the same color, gave him a true Italian look. He wore a dark blue suit with a multi-colored tie. She didn't think the jacket would actually close.

"Hello, Lorenzo. How are you my friend?" Ryan said, reaching for his hand to give it a shake before pulling him in for a man hug. "This is my new friend, Emma."

"Excellent." Lorenzo said as he nodded to Emma. "I'll find you a perfect table. And, if you don't mind, I'll sit with you for a few minutes so that you can tell me about what's going on in your life these days. I haven't seen you in a while."

"It's not my fault you weren't here when I picked up dinner last night," Ryan replied.

Emma, realizing who this was now, spoke up. "Your lasagna was fabulous. Thank you."

"What a sweet girl. Thank you for the compliment," Lorenzo stated and stepped closer to her to kiss each cheek, making Emma blush. "Very nice to meet you."

"Let's get you seated." He turned to the hostess who was now back at her station and asked what tables showed open. The girl turned the seating plan to him, and he studied it for a moment then pointed to a table so that the hostess could mark it reserved.

Turning back to Ryan, "I have the perfect table for you. Follow me." He led them through the spacious house towards the back. As they passed the open rooms, Emma noticed tables set up with white linen and a burgundy cloth over it with a floral centerpiece that held a low candle in the middle. Every room was similar, with the lighting low, heavy drapes the same color as the table accent, and dark gray carpeting. They passed what could have been a living room, a dining room, and entered another that she thought could have been a family room. Though the tables were dressed the same, this room had a fireplace that added to the warmth of the decor.

Their table was near enough to the fireplace to feel a little heat but far enough away that they didn't roast. Lorenzo held the chair out for Emma tucking the chair in as she sat. Ryan took his seat opposite her. "What can I get you to drink?" he asked Emma.

"A glass of white wine, please. A chardonnay if you have."

"Of course I have. This is no cheap Italian restaurant, you know. This is Giovanni's House and if there is something you want, we will have it," he stated proudly as his arms flailed over his head, making a point. She and Ryan both laughed at the gestures.

"And you, Ryan, the usual?" Lorenzo asked as he lit the candle on the table.

"I didn't know I had a usual," he replied smugly.

"Then it will be a surprise." Lorenzo walked off, leaving the two of them laughing. He returned moments later with Emma's white wine and a scotch on the rocks for Ryan. "I'll be back later," he said and left them.

"This place is beautiful." Emma looked around at the old paintings on the walls. She didn't recognize any of the artwork but appreciated the colors and style of them, which fit right in.

Moments later, a waiter appeared with their menus. "I'll give you a few minutes to decide," he said and strolled to another table.

Emma opened her menu and was surprised to see that there were no prices in it. "Um, how will I know what I'm paying for if there aren't any prices," she asked.

"Don't be silly, this is my treat," Ryan replied.

"You said that I could repay you with dinner."

"And here you are," he grinned. "I never once said that you had to pay for it."

"You tricked me. Are you always this sneaky?"

"Would you have said no to dinner if I said I was paying?"

"Yes. I pay my dues and I owed you for what you picked up for me today."

"Ach, such a little thing. Don't worry about it," he mumbled noting her stubbornness. They both studied the menu quietly.

The waiter approached the table. "Are you ready to order?" he asked.

"Emma, are you ready?" Ryan asked.

"Yes, I'll have the 'POLLO CON PATATE AL FORNO' please," she said in a perfect Italian accent that impressed Ryan.

"Yes madam, and a starter?" the waiter asked.

"A Caesar salad, please."

The waiter made his notes. "And you sir?"

Ryan pointed to the menu, making the waiter look over his shoulder. "The New York Strip loin for me please, medium rare."

"Yes sir, and a starter for you?"

"I'll have the same, a Caesar salad. And can you also bring us Bruschetta?"

"Right away, sir. Thank you." The waiter picked up the menues, and made his notes as he walked from the table.

"Where did you learn to speak Italian?"

"Oh, I don't speak it. I just know a few words here and there."

"But you ordered your dish in Italian. Accent and all."

"I've been to Italian restaurants before. You learn when you need to, or if you want to," she smiled.

"So, you mentioned that you were heading home?"

"Yes. I think I need more to wear besides the two pairs of jeans and the few sweaters that I brought. Girls just need their things when they stay somewhere for any length of time."

"When were you planning on going?"

"At first, I was going to go on the weekend, but Mrs. Conners is happy to spend time with Mom and she said she would spend any day with her that I wanted. I'm now considering going on Wednesday. I'll get up early and leave around seven, I think. That puts me in the city after rush hour. I can be back before dinner. I may do some shopping."

"Would you like company for the drive?"

Seeing his crooked smile gleaming at her, Emma wondered why he would offer and thought about if she wanted him with her. She was beginning to enjoy his company, but he had a way of making her feel foolish all the time. *What's the benefit?*

"Why would you want to go? It's just a quick trip. Home, pack, shop, return."

"I enjoy your company. We can get to know each other better."

"But you have work to deal with," she stated.

"Oh the joys of being the boss," he smiled. "Seriously, I see that you are an independent woman and can do everything on your own, but I'd love to drive you in so that you have time to relax. Your efforts with your mom will take a toll, so take the offer while you can," he said laughing.

Yeah, there it is. "Yes, I really don't enjoy the drive, especially in the winter. Are you sure you can get away?"

"I wouldn't offer if I couldn't."

"Then thank you. I appreciate the offer and accept."

"Wonderful. I may be tempted to drop in on my parents while you pack and shop. I'll have to check with them first."

"Sounds like a good plan. I thought you said that your parents go south for the winter?"

"They do but they always come back for Christmas. They spend a few weeks here and then leave mid-January again until about the end of March."

"I'm sure they will be happy to see you. Do you have siblings?"

"A brother. He's a couple of years older than me. His name is Luke. He works for the government and does quite well for himself. He's married, has three incredible kids already. Mia, who is eight, James is six, and Leo is three."

"How wonderful for you. You're Uncle Ryan!" She exclaimed. "I wish I had a brother or sister. My mom had trouble with my birth and couldn't have any more children. It wasn't easy growing up alone."

"An only child, huh? I hear most are spoiled rotten."

"Not this one," she laughed. "My dad was a tough man to please. He had a hard childhood and it played out the same way with me. My mom was able to keep most of his harshness from me but he was still strict."

The waiter returned to the table with their salads and the Bruschetta. They realized how hungry they were and devoured their starters. Throughout the meal, they spoke about his parents, her father, and his brother.

"Mom and Dad love to travel now. I think they are away more than they are here," he said.

Later, they ordered a desert, and as they ate, Lorenzo sat with them, telling stories of his friendship with Ryan that had Emma laughing.

"I'll never forget the first time I took you fishing with me," Lorenzo started. "He told me he was an avid fisherman," he said, looking at Emma. "We were out on the lake, early in the morning, the sun just rising. We settled into a nice quiet spot, the anchor was down. I thought it was going to be a good morning. I cast my line into the water and begin to reel it back in. This guy goes to cast his line in and the rod goes flying into the water. What does he do? He jumps in after it, rocking my aluminum boat so much that I fell backward into the lake. As I was falling over the edge, I felt a tug on my line. Gave it a good pull. I couldn't let it go. So here I am, trying to climb back into the boat with a fish pulling the line out like crazy. He's on the other side of the boat, trying to climb back in with the rod he managed to retrieve. It took us forty-five minutes to get into that boat, and reel in both lines. Needless to say, I still managed to catch one of the biggest largemouth bass that I'd ever seen. But that was the end of the fishing trip for us. We pulled up anchor and headed back, soaking wet and cold." His laugh bellowed through the room and Ryan laughed with him.

"It took me a long time to convince Lorenzo to take me fishing with him again," Ryan admitted.

"Good times, my friend, good times," Lorenzo said. "I must get back to my kitchen now." He got up and looked at Emma. "I hope you enjoyed your meal, Miss Emma."

"It was delicious, thank you. I also enjoyed your company."

"Well, thank you for that. I hope to see you back here soon." He turned to Ryan. "Bring her back, I like her," he said and walked away leaving them both laughing.

Ryan checked his watch and seeing that it was past nine-thirty, he suggested that it was time to get her back home. "We don't want to keep Mrs. Conners up too long."

"Yes, of course. I didn't realize how quickly time flew by."

Ryan called for the bill, paid it, and walked to the front entrance with Emma where he helped her with her jacket. As they stepped out of the restaurant, they felt the chill of the night.

"If you'd like, you can wait inside while I warm up the car."

"Don't be silly," she replied and ran to the SUV. He was right behind her and helped her in.

It didn't take long for the SUV to warm up and the drive back went too quickly, both thinking they didn't want the evening to end.

Ryan pulled up along the curb outside her mom's house, got out, helped her out, and walked her to the front door.

"I had a wonderful evening," she said as she fished her keys out of her purse.

"So did I. We'll have to do that again," he responded.

"Ah, here we go." She pulled the keys out and unlocked the door. "Thank you for dinner. The food and the company were fabulous."

He gave her that crooked smile and pulled her in close. "The pleasure was all mine." He looked into her eyes and saw desire. He lifted her chin with his finger and bent to kiss her but was stopped by the sudden opening of the front door. They quickly pulled apart.

"Oh, I thought I heard someone out here," Mrs. Conners stated as she stepped back from the open door, letting them in.

"Yes, we just got here," Emma said. "How is Mom doing? Did you have a good visit?"

"We had a wonderful visit. She stayed awake until just after eight o'clock. I've missed our talks so this was good for the both of us."

"I'm sure it was."

"Have you decided yet when you will be going into the city?"

"Would Wednesday be convenient for you?"

"It would and let me just say, I think it's silly for you to drive all that way, just to turn around and come back the same day. Why don't you spend the night in your own bed, I'll stay with your mom. You'll be more rested for the drive back."

"That's very kind of you to offer but I think it's manageable in one day as Ryan will be driving me in. I was hoping to leave by seven o'clock in the morning if that's all right with you."

"Perfectly fine. I'll see you on Wednesday around seven." She got her coat on, put on her boots, and looked at Ryan. "Can you run me home?"

He smiled at her. "Sure." And turning to Emma, he thanked her for her company and wished her a good night. He gave her a quick wink before stepping out the door behind Mrs. Conners.

She smiled at him, seeing the amusement in his face. Not the end to an evening that she imagined, she thought, closing the door and locking it.

She removed her jacket and boots, took her purse to the kitchen, pulled out her phone, and turned off the lights on the lower floor. She went upstairs to check on her mom and seeing that she was fast asleep and tucked in nicely, she turned off the bedside lamp and went to her own room.

Sitting herself on the bed, she sent Ryan a quick text. 'Call me when you get a moment.'

Her phone rang fifteen minutes later. "Hey, what's up?" Ryan asked.

"First, let me say thank you again. I had a good time. I also want to know if you have anyone else that can sit with my mom during the day for a bit. I don't want to put too much on Mrs. Conners," she responded.

"Sure, for when?"

"I was thinking for two hours in the afternoon so that I can go into the store and talk to Katie Simmons."

"I'll have someone there. Say about one o'clock?"

"That's perfect. It was nice of you to run Mrs. Conners home."

"It was nothing. She was chatting all the way home about how much she enjoyed the visit and what a wonderful young lady you were."

Emma laughed. "She's a nice lady as well. Okay, I'll let you go. Have a good night."

"You, too," he responded and disconnected the call.

Ryan poured himself a drink, turned on the fireplace, and some music to unwind from the day. He tipped his head back and let it rest on the back of the sofa as thoughts of Emma clouded his mind, and felt torn with his feelings.

He couldn't deny that he was deeply attracted to her. Not only did she have a natural beauty about her, she was smart, independent and a caring person. All things that made her attractive to him. When she smiled or laughed at something he said, her face glowed and her eyes sparkled.

It all seemed to be moving too fast for him, he thought, as he has only known her for a few short days.

And he couldn't help the feelings of guilt and betrayal to his wife Cathy. Even knowing that she wouldn't want him to wallow in self-pity and not get on with life, he felt unsettled. She'd be happy for him to find love again, he reasoned. They had talked about it in her last days. He took an oath that he'd never be with another woman again, and Cathy laughed and said 'get real, babe. You can't live life to the fullest without love. I know you love me, but the memory of me won't be enough. I want you to be happy. Promise me. Promise that you'll be open to loving someone again.' It had hurt him to make that promise, but he only did it to keep her happy. He knew in his heart at that time, that he'd never be able to fall in love again.

Now, eight years later, he was at odds. He felt the tug on his heart. Emma had many of the qualities that Cathy had, but she was different in her own way. Cathy counted on him to do things for her. She was more like a princess, and he loved treating her that way. Emma, on the other hand, felt the need to dig in and conquer any task, and he admired that about her. Was he ready to let this happen, he wondered.

It's only been a few days, he reminded himself. Was he a believer in love at first sight? He would have scoffed at the idea before he met Emma. But now, although it wasn't at first sight, exactly, he could see how it *could* happen.

As he thought about Cathy, the emotions of losing her ran through him once more. He sipped his drink and cried openly, missing her: her smile, her giggles, her touch, and her kisses. He missed being needed by her. He missed being able to give her everything she desired. He missed laying next to her in bed, holding her.

Ryan's tears flowed, and he did nothing to stop them. He picked up the picture of her from the mantle of his fireplace and held it close to his heart. He sat down, closed his eyes, and envisioned her dancing around the living room of the condo they had in the city, to the music she loved, singing her heart out. She had no inhibitions. And then, when both of their worlds came crashing down with her diagnosis of cancer, it seemed like the end of his life, too. Stage 4B lung cancer. He felt the guilt of not recognizing the symptoms, being an intern at the hospital.

She had a persistent cough, and she had grown weak. She insisted that it was a cold. But it didn't go away. It wasn't until she had lost a lot of weight due to a loss of appetite, and she began to spit up blood, that he implored that she get herself checked. The results of the tests destroyed them. The cancer had been so aggressive that they couldn't help her fast enough. She spent a year and a half in treatments, but it was all too late.

He held her hand through chemotherapy and radiation and watched her grow weaker and thinner. He sat with her as she took her last breath and blamed himself for all that she had been through.

Ryan's loss had been so devastating that he gave up on the idea of practicing medicine. His parents had been supportive and recommended that he take time off to recover, hoping that he'd return to being a doctor when he finished grieving.

He drove, anywhere and everywhere, and it was when he drove through the small town of Willowbrook and met Lorenzo while fishing off a dock, that he decided that this was the place he wanted to be. What he would do, he didn't know, but he was sure that something would come to him.

Now, eight years later, he'd adjusted to small-town living and was loving it. He didn't want to practice medicine but wanted to help people that needed help, so he started his own company. The best decision he'd ever made, next to marrying Cathy.

Was he ready to love again? The thought scared him. He looked at Cathy's picture once more, and it was as if she was talking to him. 'Yes, you can love again. Don't put off happiness any longer.'

"Thank you," he said to her picture and to the spirit of her that surrounded him. He put the framed photo back on the mantel, finished his drink, turned off the fire, and went to bed.

Lying in bed thinking about Emma, he knew the next few weeks were going to be difficult for her, and when her mother passes, who knows what she will do. Will she go back to the world she knows in the city? Or will something or someone entice her to stay here, he wondered.

She will be vulnerable for the next while, and he didn't want to overstep boundaries, but he needed to let her know that he cared. Maybe even give her a reason to stay in Willowbrook. It was going to be a difficult journey for her, but he'd be there to help.

Somewhere during the time he was thinking of ways to help, he drifted off, into a deep sleep.

Chapter 8

"Good morning. How are you doing today?" Emma asked with a brighter spirit. She had decided that she was going to be as happy as possible around her mom so that her mom didn't feel guilt or unhappiness in any way. Emma was determined to make her mom's last days happy ones.

She had slept in by accident and when she went to her mom's room, she wasn't there. She did a quick search of the upper level of the house and didn't find her. She ran down the stairs and discovered her sitting at the kitchen table with a cup of tea.

"I'm doing fine, dear. You are in good spirits. Must have been a good dinner date with Ryan," she smiled.

"Yes, it was lovely," Emma replied as she set about making a pot of coffee. "He took me to Giovanni's for dinner. Wonderful food there and I love the way Lorenzo fixed up the house for a restaurant. Have you been there?"

"Once, yes. With your father. He took me there for an anniversary. Very expensive though, but I agree, the food was fabulous."

"How was your visit with Mrs. Conners?"

"That woman sure can talk," Susan replied laughing. "But I enjoyed every minute with her. She brought me up-to-date on all the gossip."

"Ah, so she's a gossiper. I'll have to make sure that she's not gossiping about me."

"Too late. She's already told me about how Ryan looks at you and how you react to him."

"What do you mean? He's a nice guy. He helped me with the lights on the house and did a favor for me and for repayment he said dinner. I thought I was taking him to dinner. I didn't know he was just expecting company for dinner. He's sneaky. We're friends. That's all."

"Uh-huh. That's what they all say. But, just so that you know, I approve."

Emma laughed. "It's nothing like that, Mom. I assure you."

"So you say."

They chatted more about Julie Conners visit and that when she came over on Wednesday, they were going to play some cards. Susan talked about plans they had made for the next few weeks while they ate the light breakfast that Emma had prepared.

"And even if they don't work out, for now, I have something to look forward to," Susan said.

"Well, that all sounds good but I'm going to make sure that she knows that you need your rest, too, so that you can enjoy the things you plan to do with her."

"I know, dear. I fell asleep an hour after she arrived. I tried, but I couldn't stay awake."

"Mom, your body is still fighting and that drains you. It's perfectly natural. Sleep when you need to, everyone will understand. So, now the question, how long have you been down here? I feel bad that I slept in. I should have been here to help you."

"I've been enjoying my tea for about an hour. Don't feel guilty, I can still do some things on my own and I felt a little more energetic this morning, which is why I tackled the stairs in coming down here."

"I don't want anything to happen to you, Mom. Call me next time. I'd never forgive myself if you tried doing this on your own and you fell. So please, call me. I don't mind. Really."

"I will, next time. I promise. Now, tell me about your plans for today."

"I'm going to do some cleaning and your lunch. I wanted to head out to talk to Katie Simmons today. I'd be gone for a couple of hours. Ryan said he would have someone here with you while I'm gone so that you are not left alone. He's going to call me and let me know who it will be. I'll clear it with you before I give the OK. But I'm feeling a little guilty that I haven't spent time in the store. You are, of course, more important and Katie did say she could handle things but it was so busy there when I went in before."

"Katie is good. She can handle things and when she feels like she can't, I've given her the okay to hire anyone she wants to help her. She's done that on occasion. Not sure why she hasn't for the Christmas rush. You could ask her."

"I will and if that's the case, it's better for now if she does that while I spend my time with you. But I feel that's a conversation I need to have with her in person."

"I agree. Meet with her. I don't need anyone here. I promise to stay in bed so that you don't have to worry."

"I'd worry anyway. If you needed the bathroom like before and you didn't feel strong enough, we'd have another issue. Oh, and now that I'm thinking of it, Mom, I have a package of Depends if that's going to make you feel more comfortable. I think it's a good idea so that you don't have to stress about getting to the bathroom in time. I'll put the package in the cabinet under the sink so that you can use them whenever you need to."

"All that fuss and bother," Susan muttered. "I don't need them."

"I know, Mom, but it's more of a fuss and bother for me if I have to do laundry every couple of days because of an accident. It's perfectly normal, in your state, to lose control every once in a while. Who's going to know but you and me? Nothing to feel uncomfortable about."

"I guess you're right. Now, I am getting tired and would ask that you help me back upstairs."

"Of course. Let's get you tucked back in. Would you like to sit in the recliner or be in your bed?"

"My bed, please. It's more comfortable."

Emma helped her up from the chair, noting how frail she looked and how thin she was. Skin and bones, she thought. When she had her mom tucked back into bed, she closed the door so that she could do some cleaning in the lower half of the house without waking her.

Returning to the kitchen, she pulled her phone from her pocket and called Nisha to make sure that everything was okay at work. When Nisha reassured her that all was well, that she could forget about work for now, Emma thanked her and went to the laundry room to do some ironing.

An hour later, she received a call from Ryan stating that Julie Conners would be there at two o'clock to sit with her mom for a couple of hours.

"I didn't want to add extra to Julie's plate," Emma said to him.

"Hey, she called me. She said that she enjoyed being with your mom so much and wished she could spend more time there. I told her that you didn't want to overload her and ask too much of her. Her words, and I'm going to quote her, were 'You tell your girlfriend that I've been Susan's friend for a long time and I'm going to miss her terribly when she's gone, so I'd like to spend as much time with her as possible.' I lie not," he laughed. "So I told her to be there at two."

"Well, I'll have to thank her. She's a good friend to my mom. Mom said they had a great visit, even though it only lasted the hour she was awake. How's your day going?"

"All is good but I have to go now. I'll talk with you later so we can fix a time to leave tomorrow. Have a good day."

Before she could respond, he had disconnected the call.

When her mom woke from her nap, Emma helped her bathe and straightened the bedding before helping her back into bed. That was the one activity that wore her mother out.

At two o'clock, the doorbell rang and Julie had arrived. "I don't know how to thank you for doing this for me," Emma said.

"Nonsense. It's just as much for me. My heart breaks every time I think about losing her soon. I'm going to miss her so much," she responded and Emma hugged her. "I'd love to spend time with her every day until the time comes. This will also give you time to step away from it for a bit and take time for yourself. It isn't going to get any easier. You'll need time for yourself. Please, let me do that for you, and for me," Julie said, tears forming in the corners of her eyes.

"If that's what you want, I won't stop you, whether I go or stay, you are always welcome to visit," Emma replied. "I should go now. I need to talk to Katie about the store. I'll be back as soon as I can."

"Take your time, please. Don't hurry on my account. I'll take good care of your mom."

"I know you will, thank you." Emma put on her jacket and boots, got her purse from the kitchen, and before she stepped out, she watched Julie head up the stairs.

Main Street was busy with shoppers and deliveries in the various stores. Emma had to take two runs up and down the street with the car before she found a parking spot. The air was cold, and it was beginning to snow lightly, the feeling of Christmas was there. As she walked along the sidewalk to her mother's store, she took a few moments here and there to admire the holiday window dressings. Each uniquely different, drawing people in for a look.

She paused at a little shop of women's clothing where she spotted a robe in the window that she thought her mother would love, and made a mental note to go into the store later to get it for her.

Upon reaching the gift shop and stepping inside, she was pleased to see that it was busy. She waved to Katie and put her things in the back room. She took a moment to look around and become familiar with the way things were. Returning to the store area, she approached Katie.

"Hello, Katie. How are you?"

"Doing just fine, thank you. How's your mom doing?"

"She's hanging tough. But she's comfortable for now. I'm here to help with whatever you need."

"I'd think your time would be better spent with your mother," Katie stated coldly.

Surprised by the tone in which Katie spoke to her, Emma paused for a moment before replying, wondering what had upset Katie. "My mother has a visitor for the next couple of hours, so I thought I'd come here to give you a hand."

"Well, it is your store. You can come and go as you please. I'm fine, though."

Emma chose to make herself useful by familiarizing herself with the store, the customers, and the processes in which things happened. She took the time to talk to a few people as they came in, introducing herself and asking if they were looking for anything in particular. Everyone was friendly and mentioned that they had heard about her mom and wished her well. Most offering the kind words of 'If there's anything I can do at all…' that you say out of politeness. But she knew there were a small few who meant it.

When there was a lull in traffic, Emma approached Katie once again.

"Are you upset with me?" Emma asked.

Katie studied Emma's face for a moment. "No, sorry. I'm upset with myself. Feeling a little depressed I guess."

"Why, what's going on?"

"I'm just tired, I guess. It's a lot to be here from ten o'clock until eight o'clock every day, seven days a week."

"Why haven't you hired help? My mom said that she gave you the okay to do that when you needed to."

"Hiring someone will cut the profits to your mom. I didn't want to do that."

"Katie, you getting run down, which could lead to you becoming sick, would be even more devastating. My mom doesn't need more profits. She won't be back in the store. She's passing the store to me and I need time to think about what I'm going to do with it but the possibility is there that I may either offer you a partnership or pass it on to you completely." The look of disbelief crossed Katie's face as Emma said it.

Katie pulled the stool closer to the counter and sat down. "Seriously?"

"Yes. I think my mother would be happy knowing that you will have some part of it. You've been such a big help to her and have saved the store from going under since she can't be here anymore. Now, answer me this. If this were your store, would you hire the extra help?"

"Yes, I think I would. I'd want some downtime."

"Then do it. I'm still thinking about things, so let's just wait and see what happens, okay? We'll figure it out."

"Oh, you are a sweet girl, just like your mom says."

"Well, thank you. I thought I'd be able to come in and help you here on a daily basis but I'm about to lose my mother and I want to spend time with her during these last days. It's only a matter of time now. So, please, for now, hire someone to help you so that the burden isn't completely on you."

"Thank you, Emma, I'll go make a call right now. I think I have the perfect person in mind," Katie replied.

"All right then, you go make that call. I need to leave in about fifteen minutes. I hope you feel better about things now."

Katie stood to hug Emma. "I do, thank you." She strode off to the back room. "I'll call your mother later. I've missed chatting with her."

"You do that," Emma replied as she headed made her way to the door. On her way back to the car, she stopped in the women's clothing store where she had seen the robe earlier and purchased it in a light green color with matching slippers, and felt pleased when she left the store. She may not have much time, but she *will* have an early Christmas, she thought.

As she walked through the front door of her mother's house, she heard the laughing from the upper floor and wondered what could be so funny. She quickly put her things away and went up to investigate.

Both women were sitting in the office, her mom tucked into the recliner and Julie beside her on the love seat. They were watching TV and chatting away like best friends do. Her mom was clearly happy, and she almost hated to interrupt them to let them know she had returned.

They both burst out laughing once again as Emma walked through the door. They looked at her in surprise as she took a seat next to Julie and watched the episode of Seinfeld with them. Fifteen minutes later, it was over and all three had had a good laugh.

"I don't normally watch Seinfeld re-runs but that was great," Emma declared.

"You should watch all the re-runs. It'll keep you laughing for hours. They currently have a Seinfeld marathon going on so if you find yourself with nothing to do, that would be the thing to do." Julie said.

"I've never watched Seinfeld either but now I know what I missed," Susan chimed in.

"Well, you're back and I should head home. I'll be here with you all day tomorrow," Julie said to Susan. "We can watch more if you're up to it." She gave Susan's cheek a quick kiss. "You get some rest tonight. Would you like me to help you back to bed?"

"Thank you, Julie. I'll be fine. I'm going to watch the next episode and then maybe head off to my bed again." Susan responded.

"I'll see you tomorrow."

"I'm just going to go down with Julie, I'll be right back," Emma said to her mom and left the room with Julie.

Once they got to the front door, Julie commented that it was difficult to see her friend slipping away bit by bit and understood the need to step away from it a bit to recharge.

"You're a brave soul to be able to be here and help your mom."

"I'm doing what she did for me for so many years. There comes a time when a daughter needs to take care of her mom and I'm honored to have that opportunity."

"You're a good girl. I'll see you at seven."

"Thank you so much, Mrs. Conners. I'm so grateful that my mom has you."

"Good night, dear one." Julie responded, touching Emma cheek before she stepped out the door.

Emma went back to the office and checked on her mom. She was fast asleep in the recliner and Emma left her there. She went down to fix a light meal so that when her mom woke up, it would be ready.

It was six o'clock when she thought she heard her mom. She carried the tray upstairs with their dinners and placed it on the table.

"You dozed off," Emma said.

"I guess I did. I'm very tired."

"Well, eat a little bit and I'll get you tucked into bed."

She watched as her mom nibbled on a bit of food. She noted that her mom didn't eat much and hoped it was enough to get some nourishment into her body. She then helped her mom back into bed, tucked her in and settled herself in the family room. She turned on the fire, poured herself a glass of wine and cried. *Damn, this is hard.*

When Ryan called later that evening, she kept the conversation short.

"I'm tired, Ryan, we can chat tomorrow if you're still up to driving? If not, I'll understand and go on my own."

"Of course I'm going to drive you in. We'll chat tomorrow. Go to bed. Get some sleep. You obviously need it."

"Thanks, Ryan. Good night. See you at seven." She disconnected the call. Good advice, she thought, and turned off the fire, washed and put away her wine glass, and went up to bed.

Chapter 9

Emma's' alarm clock beeped at 5:45 a.m. and she quickly turned it off so that it didn't wake her mom. After showering and changing, she went to her mother's room and saw she was still fast asleep. She chose to let her sleep and went down to the kitchen.

She made a list of things for Julie Conners: Light Breakfast should be, eggs, tea, and toast, Lunch-- soup of her choice, and hopefully she'd be back to prepare dinner. She indicated on the note where things were

There was a light knock at the door at five minutes to seven. Emma opened it and let Julie in. She was surprised at the large bag that she carried.

"Good morning. How is your mom doing?"

"I don't know yet, she's still sleeping."

"That's all right, let her sleep. I'll go up in a bit and wait in the office until she wakes. I've brought some games for us today and I baked last night so there are some goodies in here for her as well," she said holding up the bag.

"I'm hoping to be back before dinner and left you a note on where things were and what she might like for breakfast and lunch."

"Dear, I've known your mom a while now. I know where she keeps things and what she likes. You worry too much, we will be fine. And if you don't make it back before dinner, that's not an issue. If you don't make it back tonight, that's not an issue, just let me know. You go and don't worry. Do what you need to do. Your mom is in good hands."

"Yes, I'm sure she is. How can I ever thank you?"

"No thanks needed, dear."

There was another light knock at the door and Emma opened it to Ryan.

"Good morning, Emma, Mrs. Conners."

"Good morning to you, too. Now go. Have a safe drive. All is well here." Julie said to Emma.

"Are you ready?" Ryan asked.

"Just need to grab my purse," she replied.

At ten after seven, they were turning onto the highway, heading south to the city. It was a cold morning and Ryan had turned on the seat warmers in his SUV. He had the radio on a low volume in an attempt to listen for traffic reports as they got closer to the city.

"So, how was your day yesterday?" he asked.

"Good, long, tiring," she said with a half laugh. "Helping Mom bathe gets more and more difficult as she just doesn't have the energy anymore."

"Give her a sponge bath instead."

"What?"

"Try the tub bath twice a week but do the other days with a sponge bath. It's not like she's getting dirty because she's out and about, it's more to just remove any body perspiration and freshen her up so that she feels better."

"That does sound like a good idea. Why didn't I think about that. I'll try that and see how she feels about it."

"If that doesn't work for her, let me know, I think I have something that will help her. What else?" he asked.

"I went to see Katie at the store in the afternoon. Her attitude seemed quite cold to me when I first got there, so I just kept myself busy with customers until there was a lull. Then I approached her and asked what was wrong. She told me how tired she was, taking care of the store for so many hours a day, seven days a week. I convinced her to hire someone to help her. I wish I could help her but I want to spend as much time as possible with Mom. She understood that. I think we came to an agreement with things, so that's better now. She was heading off to call someone when I left."

"It's good you went in then. I can understand, with the Christmas rush, how she would feel run down. She should have had help in there a long time ago."

"I know, right? My mom had given her the okay to hire someone long ago. She told me she didn't want to cut my mom's profits. I said why not? She doesn't need the profits. I mean, let's get real, she can't take it with her."

"You're right. And if she gets that run down, she's going to get sick, and then the store would be closed. That's not good either."

"Exactly what I told her."

"Oh, I forgot to ask, do you want to stop and get a coffee?"

"That would be wonderful, thank you."

Ryan pulled off the next off-ramp to find a Tim Horton's drive-through for coffee. Once they had their coffees and breakfast bagels, they were on the road again.

"How long do you think it will take you to pack up your things?" Ryan asked. "I just want to know how much time I have to visit with Mom and Dad."

"Oh, take whatever time you need. I can do it in a half-hour or 3 hours. It doesn't matter to me."

"Well, how about this then. We get you all packed up first, then I'll take you to meet my parents. We could go to lunch somewhere then do whatever shopping you need to before we head back."

"I don't think I should intrude on your visit with your parents."

"You wouldn't be an intrusion. I'm sure they'd be happy to meet you."

"Well, that sounds good then. But only if they are okay with me being there."

"Let me give them a call." He pushed a button on his steering wheel, requesting a connection to Jeff Campbell. The phone rang a couple of times before a male voice answered.

"Good morning, Ryan. Are you on your way?"

"Good morning, Dad. Yes, we are. I've talked to Emma about this, we'd like to meet you and Mom for lunch somewhere. You can meet Emma then. Is that alright with you?"

"We'd love to meet your girlfriend."

Emma could feel her face get red from embarrassment.

"I'll let that go, Dad," he said with a bit of a laugh. "How about we meet at Donatello's at noon."

"Sounds good. I'll go tell your mom when she gets off the phone with your brother."

"Thanks, Dad. See you later."

"Drive safe. You've got precious cargo in your vehicle." The call disconnected.

"I think he likes you already," Ryan laughed.

"Um, I don't even know what to say to that," she laughed. "You told them I'm your girlfriend?"

"No, but you are the first woman that I'm taking home to meet my parents since Cathy's passing."

"That's eight years. Haven't you had a relationship since then?"

"No, and I haven't desired to have one either. I'm quite fine on my own."

Emma sat quietly as she pondered what he had said. *Does that mean he's not wanting to get involved?* She had such an attraction to him, not just physically but in the more important ways. He was a good man, and she was near ready to lose her heart to him, as early as it was in the relationship.

"Well, then you'll just have to set him straight when you see him. Let him know we are just friends and you are helping me out."

Ryan felt a small stab to the heart. He knew that he wanted more this time. More with her, but she obviously didn't feel the same way.

"I'm sorry if it embarrassed you. I'll talk to him," he replied. "What about you? Are you in a relationship?"

"No. Haven't desired to be either," *Until you*, she thought.

"Why would a beautiful woman like you want to be single?"

"Because, to put it bluntly, most men are assholes."

"Ouch."

"Really, most just want what they want, when they want, and if they can't get, they're gone."

"Again, ouch," he said.

"Look, I know there are some good ones out there, I just haven't found one yet. I was engaged once but caught him cheating. I haven't really dated since."

"I thought I was a good man. Everyone says so," he said sheepishly.

"Yeah, you are one of the exceptions which is the only reason why I said *most* men and not every man." Emma was afraid of where this conversation was going and changed the subject, asking about Donatello's restaurant.

They rode the rest of the way making small talk. Both were a little bothered by the conversation after the call to his father. They listened to music and the news and had some quiet moments in between. When they reached the city, near ten o'clock, Emma directed him to her condo. He parked the SUV in a visitor's parking spot and escorted her to the sixth floor. Once inside her condo, she headed straight for the kitchen.

"Can I get you a drink?"

"Sure, what do you have."

"Pop, water, juice, take a peek in the fridge," she replied, putting her purse on the little glass kitchen table in the corner, then going to the sink to wash her hands. It was a habit she formed years ago, and now it was second nature.

Ryan pulled out a pop, popped the tab, and took a sip, as he looked around. "Nice place you have here. Very modern, open, and bright."

"Yes, thank you. I don't like living in dark spaces. I like the whites, with color accents or light cream colors with earth tone accents. Old houses are nice with the wood panels, dark floorings, and such, but just not for me. I need light in my life."

"I understand. Original paintings?" he asked, pointing to the two framed pictures on the back wall of her dining room.

"Yes, as a matter of fact, they are. Do you like them? I know we don't all have the same taste in art, just curious on your thoughts."

"Actually, I do. The colors work well together. It's just..." he paused.

"Just what?"

"Well, I don't mean this in a bad way, but they don't go together."

She looked at the paintings again. One of a field of wildflowers, the other of a sunset in the mountains. "Yes, I know. I didn't have another wall to hang one, so they both ended up here. One day, I'll have a bigger place and they can have their own wall," she laughed. "I've got 4 more in the bedroom, would you like to see them?"

"I would." They walked into the bedroom together and Ryan's eyes immediately went to a painting of a lake, serene, calm water with a bit of mist rising from it. It was early morning, a small fishing boat, and two people in the boat, one reeling in a fish that was jumping. Splashes of water coming off the fish.

"I love this," he said, pointing at it. He walked towards it and looked at the artist's name. He was stunned for a moment and turned to her. "You did these?"

"Just a little hobby when I have time."

"Your paintings are wonderful. But this one is my favorite. Do you sell your stuff?"

"No, I'm not that good."

"Are you kidding me? You have talent, girl. You just don't know it. I bet you in a small town like Willowbrook you could sell these easily."

"See, I'm not that good."

"What do you mean?" he asked in confusion.

"Well, you said, I could sell these easily in a small town."

"Yes, that's because in a large city like this, it would be harder to get your work into galleries. Still possible, but harder."

She laughed. "I know what you meant. I just wanted to see if you could talk your way out of a slip of the tongue," she smiled at him.

He put his pop down on the bedside table and walked over to her. "Testing me, are you? Well, bring it on, girl. I'll prove I'm a good guy."

"I already know you are."

He reached out and held her shoulders, pulled her in, and was ready to kiss her, but she stepped back.

"I think I should start packing." She moved to her walk-in closet and opened the door. "So, tell me why you like that painting so much?"

Feeling like he just got snubbed, he turned away from her grabbed his pop can, and headed to the bedroom door. "I like what it portrays. It's has a calming effect. I like that. I know that sense of tranquility. Been there, done that."

"Yeah, my dad loved to fish. I did that one after he passed away."

"It's beautiful, Emma. I'll go wait in the living room while you pack." He stood by the window overlooking the neighborhood and thought about what happened. Was he being pushy, he wondered. The conversation they had earlier still had him feeling uneasy. He knew he would have to address this at some point. Now was not the time.

She came out twenty minutes later with a suitcase and a large art transport bag.

"What's in there?" Ryan pointed to the bag.

"I thought I'd take a couple of canvases and my paints to Mom's so that I can paint when the mood strikes. Not much else to do there when she's sleeping in the evenings. It'll keep me busy. Do you have room for it in the car?"

"Of course I do. Do you have everything you need?" He checked his watch, it was approaching eleven o'clock.

"Yes, I believe I have enough clothes now. Whatever I don't have, I can buy there but this does save me a lot of money," she smiled.

"Let me take that then and we can be on our way to meet my parents." He grabbed the suitcase from her hands and reached for the art bag.

"I'll take that if you don't mind. Are you done with your pop?"

"Yes, thank you."

Emma took the empty pop can to the kitchen, rinsed it, and put it in the garbage. Tucking her purse under her arm, and grabbing her keys and the art bag, they left, locking the door behind them. Once they settled into the SUV, he turned to her.

"Did I say something to upset you?"

"No, why do you ask?"

"Just a feeling. Okay, let's go."

He drove skillfully to the core of the city, avoiding three potential accidents on the way.

Ryan escorted Emma through the doors of Donatello's and spotted his parents at a booth right away. He helped Emma off with her jacket and walked with her to where his parents sat, hanging both their jackets on the hook, on the back of the booth seat.

His father got up, shook Ryan's hand, and gave him a pat on the back. "Nice to see you son." Then turning to Emma, he extended his hand. "What a pleasure it is to meet you. Ryan has told us about you."

"Emma, this is my father, Jeff Campbell, and my mother, Ann. Hello mother," Ryan said and Anne blew a kiss to him.

Emma felt a little embarrassed but shook his hand and greeted both parents. "Lovely to meet you both." She slipped into the booth.

"We're sorry to hear that your mom isn't doing well. Ryan has filled us in on what's going on. If we can be of any help, please, don't hesitate to ask," Ann said sympathetically, putting her hand over Emma's on the table.

"Thank you, that's very kind," Emma replied, trying to hold her emotions in tack.

The waiter came over, dropped menus on the table, took their drink order, and left again.

Seeing that Emma was in an emotional state, Jeff changed the subject to let her collect herself and turned his attention to Ryan. "So, tell me what's going on in your neck of the woods."

"Nothing much, Dad. The business is doing well which makes me feel sad because that indicates that there are a lot of people in Willowbrook and its surrounding area that are incapacitated in some way. Believe it or not, there are some days when I wish that my business did poorly because that would mean everyone is well. Pipe dream, I know. It just gets hard sometimes."

"I'm sure it does and I understand your sentiment. But, I'm glad you are doing well with it."

"I'm thinking about expanding the business into the next town. Start small scale and build as needed. If I can do that through the northern area, even franchise the business, then I'll be set. What do you think?"

"Sounds like a great idea. Profitable for sure. Everyone needs help."

"I still have to work out the details. How are Brian and family doing? Haven't heard from him for a while."

Ann spoke up. "That's your own fault. You should call him more often. He'll be at the house for Christmas."

"Good. Can't wait to see the brats." Ryan laughed. "And when do you plan on going south again?"

The waiter had arrived with drinks, taken their orders, and was off once more.

"Not until mid-January. We've booked a cruise that will take us to St. Lucia where we will stay for three weeks. Then we catch a cruise ship that takes us to Florida where we will stay until the end of March. We have one more cruise at the end of March, going to Panama. It stops at the ABC islands first. I've never been through the canal. From there, we fly home," Ann said.

"Wow, that's an incredible trip," Emma exclaimed.

"We love to travel," Ann replied. "Not this summer, but next, we will go to Europe. I've never done a riverboat cruise and it looks wonderful. Just haven't decided yet which one."

"I've looked at cruises, I've never been on one. It can't be very enjoyable to do that by yourself."

"Oh, I wouldn't say that. You meet so many people and you can do anything you want on your timetable," she laughed.

As the women chatted about cruising, the men discussed the possibilities of franchising Ryan's business. They talked through their meal and when they were done, Jeff tried to address Emma once more.

"I know you are going through a very difficult time right now. I can't imagine what it's like for you but know this. My son is a good man and will help you in any way he can and if he screws up, I want you to call me and I'll be there to help you. You are a delightful young lady and it's been our pleasure to get to know you."

"Dad, I'm not going to screw up. I'm committed to helping Emma in any way that she needs." Ryan cut in.

"Thank you so much for the kind words. I appreciate the offer, truly. I've enjoyed getting to know both of you as well," Emma replied.

"Well, son, your mother and I need to get going. We have some shopping to do and I'm sure you will want to get back to your mother," he directed to Emma.

"Yes."

Jeff called for the bill, paid it, and they all slipped out of the booth, put on their coats, and left together. Once the goodbye hugs were given, they walked away in opposite directions.

"Your mom and dad are wonderful people. Thank you for letting me meet them," Emma said, pulling her collar up on her jacket. The air temperature felt colder.

"Yeah, I'm happy with them," he replied smugly. "Where to?"

Emma told him what she was looking for, and they shopped for another hour before heading back north. It was three-thirty when they got on the highway and traffic was starting to build.

"I don't know how to thank you for all that you've done for me today. It's truly appreciated," Emma started.

"No thanks needed. I said I would help."

"Yes, I know, but you are taking so much time away from your business and your personal life to help me."

"Hey, I got to see my parents because of you. I should be thanking you," he laughed. "Now that I think about it, there is something you can do to thank me."

"You name it."

"I want you to take some personal time Friday night. Let's have dinner together. I'm sure you will need it by then."

Emma thought about it for a moment. Is he helping her step away or is this for personal reasons? He had said he was fine on his own. He said he hasn't desired to have a relationship. She didn't want to build up any hopes. Distance was more appropriate.

"You don't have to do that. I can step away from things when I get to painting again. That will help me a great deal."

"I know I don't have to, I want to. It's just as good for me as it is for you. I enjoy your company."

"All right then, Friday for dinner it is." They chatted about his parents for the rest of the way north and when they reached Emma's mom's house, he helped her with the suitcase and bags while she carried the art bag. She had barely gotten through the door when Julie came rushing down the stairs.

"I'm glad you are back. I wasn't sure what I should do," she said frantically.

"Why, what's wrong?" Emma replied with concern.

"Your mom seems to have taken a turn for the worse in the past twenty minutes. She's having difficulty breathing."

"I'll go up right now and see her," Emma said, dropping what she had on the floor. In a panic, she raced up the stairs and found her mom, lying on her back, breathing with great difficulty.

"Mom, can I get you anything? Do you want to sit up?"

"I can't breathe."

"I'm going to ask Ryan to come up. He can help."

Her mother nodded. Emma called Ryan from the top of the stairs. "Ryan, can you come up, please. We need you."

A moment later, Ryan was in the bedroom and Julie had followed him up. "I'm sure she needs to be put on oxygen. Call the hospital and clear it with them. I'll run and get what's needed."

Emma called the hospital and with tears running down her face, she explained who she was and what was happening. They asked her to take her mother's blood pressure, and she was thankful that she had purchased a new BP monitor for that reason. She retrieved it from one of the bags that she had dropped in the hallway and took the reading while the nurse waited on the other end of the line. When she gave the reading to the nurse, she was put on hold for a moment.

"This is Dr. Evans. You should bring your mother into the hospital." A female voice came from the other end of the phone connection.

"Hello, Dr. Evans. My mother has stage 4 cancer and was sent home to die. She didn't want to die in the hospital. What can I do to help her breathe? It's very labored."

"We would normally put the patient on oxygen."

"That's what I wanted to know," Emma cut in. "I have someone going to get that for her."

"This is a clear sign that she is getting close. Does she have any medication that she's taking right now?"

Emma gave her the name of the container with pills, sitting on her night table.

"That is a pain killer. Give her that as needed. Other than that, if she's not willing to come into the hospital, there isn't much we can do."

"Thank you. I have Ryan Campbell helping me, don't know if you know him. He's advising but asked me to clear the oxygen with you first."

"Yes, I do know him and I'm glad you have his help. He knows what he's doing because he has the background. You're in good hands but let us know if there's anything else you need."

"Thank you. I will." She disconnected the call. Julie hugged her, hoping it would help.

Ten minutes later, Ryan was coming up the stairs. He didn't knock this time, knowing there was no time to spare. He set up the machine, put the mask on Susan's face, and watched to make sure she was receiving the oxygen.

When Emma's mom's breathing began to level out and the blood pressure readings leveled out, they quietly left her to rest.

Downstairs, in the kitchen, Emma had a hard time putting her emotions back in check. They sat at the kitchen table and Julie fixed a pot of coffee for them.

"I'm forever thanking you, Ryan. You've come to my aid so many times now. Thank you," Emma said.

"It's not going to be long now," Ryan replied. "I'm going to set you up with a nurse practitioner who will come in and check her vitals twice a day. She will also administer any medication that your mom needs in order to be comfortable. I'll make that call now," he said getting up from the table and going into the den.

"It's so hard to watch," Julie said, placing a mug of coffee in front of Emma. "I'm glad you came home when you did."

"I think we need to remember Mom's wishes. When it's time, we need to let her go, as difficult as that will be. Thank you so much for staying with her."

"I wish I could do more. I'm sorry you had to come home to this."

Ryan came back into the kitchen and Julie got up to get his coffee. "It's all set. Erica Tillings will be here tomorrow around eight to check your mom. Be sure to get her number when she arrives so that you can call her if you need to."

"That name sounds familiar," Emma stated. She got up from the table, "be right back." She ran up the stairs and pulled the file folder from the desk drawer that her mom had her go through. When she opened it, her name was on the front of the folder. She took the folder down to the kitchen with her.

"Mom left me this. She asked me to call the nurse's number on the front cover when the time came near. It's the same name as what you just gave me. She's also prepared everything for her death." She handed the folder over to Ryan. "I can't think straight. Is there anything else that you can think of that I need to do when she passes that you think I may need to talk to her about?"

Ryan took a quick look through the folder, feeling a little like he was intruding on privacy. "No, I think she's got it all covered. This will make it easier for you, Emma. Your mom was thinking of you when she did this."

Emma pulled a tissue from her pocket and wiped the tears from her face and her nose. They sat an hour longer, trying to comfort one another before both Ryan and Julie left.

"I'm just two doors down. Call me anytime you need me," Ryan reminded her in the entrance hallway.

"And I'm just up the street a bit. You can call me, too. Anytime, day or night," Julie stated.

"Thank you. Both of you."

Emma picked up her suitcase and carried it up the stairs and put the rest of the items away. She stepped back into her mom's room and sat in the chair and cried silently.

Chapter 10

The clock on the night table, beside her mom's bed, showed 4:10 a.m. Emma had fallen asleep in the chair and awoke startled when she heard her mom move. The room was still dimly lit because the lamp had not been turned off.

"Good morning. Can I get you anything?"

Her mom tried to remove the oxygen mask and Emma helped her so that she could speak. "I feel wet again," she said in a raspy voice.

"That's okay, Mom, I'll get you cleaned up. Do you think you can get up?"

"No, dear. I know I can't."

"That's all right. I'm going to help you off with your nightie and take off the Depends that you are wearing. Then I'll help you to Dad's side of the bed and we can get you changed into dry clothes and I'll change the sheets. How does that sound?"

"Thank you, Emmie."

Emma went about doing what she had said, all the while making sure that her mom was warm and comfortable. She noted that her mom's feet were bluish and cold. When she was done, she laid an extra blanket over her Susan's feet, she carried the soiled nightie and linens to the laundry hamper that now sat outside the bedroom, and returned to her mom's side.

"Come, lie down beside me," Susan requested.

Emma did as requested, lying on her father's side of the bed. She snuggled close to her mom.

"It's time, Emmie. I feel it."

"Don't say that, Mom. We haven't had enough time."

"Your dad is waiting for me. He told me so."

"You tell Dad to wait. I still need you here."

"He's waited a long time, Emmie. I need to be with him. I don't want to prolong this anymore. It's too hard."

Emma cried, holding on to her mom. "It's too soon, Mom. It's happening too fast. You can't go yet," she wailed.

"I love you, Emmie. I can't hold on any longer. We will be watching over you. Your dad says that he loves you, too, and misses you. And if you listen closely, you will be able to hear us in the silence of the night."

"I love you, too, and Dad. I miss him, too," she cried. It was quiet for a few minutes before Emma realized that her mom had passed.

"No!" she screamed, as she sat up. "Don't leave yet!"

She shook her mom gently a couple of times and knew at that point there was nothing she could do. She cried, holding her mom in her arms, feeling that desperate need to bring her back. Instantly, she missed her. Instantly, she felt the stinging pain of grief. The river of tears flowed as she sobbed over her mother's body. She regretted having left her to go to the city. She regretted not having visited her more through the last few years. She regretted not having called her more often. She regretted having given her mom a hard time when she was a teen.

"I'm so sorry, Mom," she repeated over and over as she rocked her mom. "So sorry."

It was six in the morning before she was able to put her mother's limp body back down. She got up from the bed, tucked her in to keep her warm, and went to call Ryan.

"Emma? Are you okay?" he asked.

"She's gone," was all she could say.

"I'm on my way over." He disconnected the call.

Emma went downstairs to open the door when the bell rang. Ryan stepped in and immediately pulled her in for a hug, and she sobbed once more. He spoke to her softly, trying to soothe her, rocking side to side, letting her sob for as long as she needed to.

"I'm so sorry, Emma," he said quietly. "She's with your dad now and pain-free. She loved you very much, and I know you being here with her helped her pass peacefully." He kissed the top of her head, wishing he could take her grief from her. It hurt him to see her suffer.

When the sobs eased, she backed away. "I don't know what to do now," she stated as she looked at Ryan who stood in-front of her with disheveled hair, wearing a white t-shirt and grey jogging pants. He hadn't even taken the time to put on a jacket.

"Let me go up and just check to see if there are any vital signs at all."

"I can't go back up there," she said.

"I know. You stay here. Put on a pot of coffee and we'll talk about the next steps. I'll go up on my own."

She nodded and went into the kitchen as he headed up the stairs.

Five minutes later, he sat at the kitchen table with Emma. "I called Erica Tillings, she's on her way over. She needs to fill out the paperwork so that your mom can go to the funeral home. Do you know what time she passed away?"

"I fell asleep in the chair next to her bed. I heard her move at 4:10. I saw the clock as soon as I opened my eyes. She had messed the bed. She was too weak to get up, so I rolled her over to the other side of the bed, once I got her nightie off. I gave her a fresh nightie, changed the sheets, and put her back on her side. She asked me to lie down beside her. We talked for a few minutes and then she was gone." She cried once more. "Just like that."

"So, I'm guessing it took about twenty minutes for you to get her comfortable again and then a bit of a chat. I'm going to put her time of death at about four-forty five a.m. Does that sound right?"

"Yes, I think so."

"Why didn't you call me earlier?"

"I needed to be with her."

"I understand." He got up, poured two mugs of coffee, and sat down again, placing a mug in front of her. He reached for the folder that was still lying on the kitchen table. "Can I take a look at this again?"

She nodded, wiping tears from her face. He opened the folder, flipped through the pages, and noted that everything that needed to be done, had been done. Her mother had left a list of friends that should be notified upon her death.

"I'll call Julie in a couple of hours. She can take the list of your mom's friends and call them to let them know. We can tell her that after funeral arrangements have been made, someone will update them," Ryan said. "If you'd like to make that call, that's up to you. I don't know how much you'll be able to handle."

He studied her face. Eyes red and swollen and her skin looked pale. It appeared like she could use sleep.

"Emma, why don't you go up and close your eyes for a while. Get some sleep. I'll stay down here and call the funeral home to come and get your mom, once Erica has been here. I'll take care of things," he said, putting his hand over hers on the table.

"I don't think I can sleep right now," she replied.

"Then just go lie down and rest. Either upstairs or down here in the family room. I can light a fire."

She looked at him with lost puppy eyes, wondering what she did to deserve such a good friend. She nodded and said that she would lie down in the family room. He lit the fire, got her a blanket, and left her to rest.

Half an hour later, Erica came through the door. Emma was fast asleep and Ryan took her upstairs to Susan. She spent a few minutes checking vital signs and filled out the paperwork, indicating the four forty-five time of death as per the conversation Ryan had with Emma.

"This just happened too quickly. Up until yesterday, she only showed signs of weakness, fatigue, and a loss of appetite. Emma and I were in the city yesterday. A friend stayed with Susan. When we got back, she was having difficulty breathing. I hooked her up right away to the oxygen. I expected at least a week before she passed. I've never seen this happen so quickly before."

"When I spoke with her weeks back and she told me her wishes, one of the things she stated strongly was that she was ready to go. She wanted to be with her husband," she paused for a moment. "She knew she was fighting a losing battle. If the will to live isn't there anymore, the fight loses it's strength. The battle is over quicker."

"I guess. Can you prescribe a sedative for Emma? She may need it over the next little bit."

"I can write a script but before she has it filled, ask if she's allergic to anything. Or have her discuss this with the pharmacist."

"Will do."

Erica completed and signed the paperwork and handed a copy to Ryan along with a script for a sedative for Emma.

"I'll call the funeral home to come and get her as soon as they open," Ryan said.

He showed Erica out after thanking her again and waited in the kitchen for Scott's Funeral Home to open. He pulled out his phone and scrolled through social media until seven o'clock. He called the funeral home and spoke to Ian, someone he'd come to know over the last eight years.

Ryan announced that Susan Jones had passed away this morning and that Erica had been out to fill out and sign the paperwork. He requested that the body be picked up as soon as possible.

Ian explained to Ryan that Susan had made all the arrangements of what she wanted with casket and funeral service, and he would arrange a date and time for the funeral and was sending someone right over for the body.

When the doorbell rang again, Emma woke. She saw Ryan sitting in the chair, just opening his eyes. "That's the funeral home, come to get your mother," he said.

She got up right away and as she headed for the stairs, she called out, "I just need another moment with her."

Ryan opened the door to two men with a gurney. He let them in stating that Susan was on the upper floor. He would take them up.

When they reached the top floor, Emma was kneeling beside the bed in silent prayer. She looked drained when she finished and invited the men in to take her mother. "Please, be careful," she said and felt stupid for saying it immediately after.

Once they left, Ryan sat with Emma for a bit before stating that he had to leave. "I'll check in with you later. I can drop off the list of your mom's friends to Julie's and let her know if you like so that she can call them."

"Yes, I think that would be good. I need time," she simply stated.

He got up and retrieved the list from the kitchen table.

"Wait, let me take a picture of the list so that I have a copy." He set the paper down, and she pulled her phone from her pocket and took the picture. "Thank you, Ryan, for being here for me this morning. I don't know what I would have done without you."

He pulled her in for a hug. "I'll always be here for you." He wanted to kiss her. The urge was strong and demanding, but he knew how fragile she was right now and resisted those feelings with all he had.

He picked up the paper once more and went to the front door. "Call me if you need anything."

She nodded and watched as he stepped out, locking the door behind him.

Emma made the necessary calls that day, to the lawyer, the funeral home for the date they had available for the service, and she spoke to Julie. It was to be a small service in the local Anglican Church and a few words at the cemetery.

She didn't want to talk to anyone or see anyone. She wasn't ready. She left everything up to Julie and trusted that she would make all the right choices.

Emma saw that Ryan had called a number of times, but she didn't want to answer, instead, she sent him a text, thanking him for his concern, she needed to be alone.

Chapter 11

On the day of her mother's funeral, Emma put on the black dress that she had purchased while in the city and stood in front of the mirror and cried. She tried covering the dark shadows under her eyes with make-up, hoping it would help and gave a bit of color to her face. As she stood by the front door getting ready to leave for the church, it suddenly occurred to her that she should have talked to Julie so that she knew what was going on. Now she regretted the lack of communication.

With her coat wrapped tightly around her, black scarf around her neck, she opened the door to leave and was shocked to see Ryan standing there. Her shoulders dropped in resignation. "Why are you here?" she asked.

"I came to take you to the church. You shouldn't be going on your own."

"That's kind of you, Ryan, but I could have done this on my own, by myself."

"Yes, I know you *could* have. You are one of the strongest women I know. I'm here for support. Let me take you."

Emma didn't want to argue with him, so she agreed. She was surprised to see a limousine sitting in front of the house. It was to be her first ride in one. Ryan helped her in and climbed in beside her.

When they got to the church, he helped her out of the limo and walked with her inside. They entered a side door where Julie greeted them.

Julie threw her arms around Emma. "I've been so worried about you. I've knocked at your door a few times. Are you all right?"

"Thank you, Julie, I'm fine, and thank you for arranging all this for me. My mom was right, I wouldn't have been able to handle the decisions that needed to be made. I have two major ones left to make and have no idea how to decide."

"Well, you let me know if I can help. Now, let me give you a rundown on what is about to happen and then I'll introduce you to the priest that will do the service." They moved off together, talking about the proceeding. There was to be a viewing for an hour before the service, at which point the coffin would be moved into the church. She would follow, taking a seat in the front pew and the priest would give his sermon and a friend wanted to give a eulogy.

When it came time, Emma was ushered into an area where her mom lay in the coffin she wanted, and she could feel her knees weakening as she approached it. Ryan quickly held onto her, wrapping an arm around her waist, giving her the support she needed. She had a few moments with her mother before others were let into the room and quietly said their goodbyes.

Emma put on a strong face as she stood close to the coffin, listening, but not comprehending, to strangers giving their condolences as they passed by her. She tried her best to thank them and remember their names. She was surprised at the turnout, many strangers, and thankfully, a few others that she knew.

Ryan's parents had come, hugging her and letting her know that she could count on them for anything she needed. Some people from her office had arrived, including Nisha and her boss who told her to take her time coming back. Katie had closed the store for the day and paid her respects. Even Lorenzo was there telling her that if she came into his restaurant, she was to ask for him, and he'd make sure that the next meal was on him. She wiped at the corners of her eyes occasionally as the tears started to build. Ryan stood by her side the whole time, making sure she was okay.

The coffin was closed and moved into the church with the flowers before the guests were asked to find their seats for the sermon. The flowers were arranged around the coffin that now had the lid closed and her mom's picture on top surrounded with a spray of roses. The organ music played as they all found their seats.

Emma and Ryan entered right before the priest, and he sat in the front row with her. The priest spoke of everlasting life. Emma was not a churchgoer but had listened to a few sermons, for other reasons, that were downright boring. This one seemed special to her, and she felt good about it. A hymn was sung by a small choir as the priest passed the space of the pulpit to a gentleman that was going to give the eulogy.

He stood behind the pulpit and talked about her mother. He mentioned things that she had never known about her, and it brought tears which she tried to wipe away as guilt washed over her. Ryan reached for her hand, squeezing it in support.

When the eulogy was done, the choir and the organ started again. The priest walked down the aisle to the front doors. The pallbearers carried the coffin following him and Ryan and Emma right behind. Once outside, the coffin was loaded into a hearse, and Emma and Ryan got into the waiting limo behind it. Emma didn't expect many to be at the cemetery and was surprised at the turnout. A few words were said by the priest before the coffin was lowered into the grave that had been opened beside her father. Before people said their goodbyes to

Emma, Lorenzo spoke up, inviting anyone that wanted to join them at Giovanni's would be welcomed for a celebration of Susan Jones' life.

Emma was floored by the invitation and went to him, thanking him for this. He held her face in his hands and said, "Sweetheart, anything for you," and smiled at her before giving her a hug.

Many chose not to follow to Giovanni's but the few that did, represented the closest of her mother's friends and support for her. Lorenzo had the place set up with pictures of her mom in each room. Tables had been pushed back so that people could mingle. Flowers were placed throughout the rooms and servers carried trays of food while serene music played in the background.

Emma walked through each room, studying the pictures. Many of which she had never seen before and with people she didn't recognize. She was happy to see her father in some of the pictures. Her heart felt heavy.

"How?" she asked Lorenzo. "How did you do this? Where did you get all the pictures?"

"Sweetheart, your mother was loved. We put a notice in the paper asking for anyone with pictures of her or your father to bring them here. They are on loan for you and for others to enjoy as they mingle and chat about her, about your parents. I'm glad it all came together. She was loved."

"Thank you, Lorenzo. You have a special place in my heart," Emma stated and kissed his cheek.

Ryan stood with his parents, only steps away and overheard the conversation and when she made that statement to Lorenzo, he felt a stab to his heart.

Emma did her best to mingle with the group for a while but felt drained after a couple of hours. She needed to go home. She said her goodbyes to all that were still there and headed to the door, pulling her phone from her purse.

"Where are you going?" Ryan asked as he followed her to the door.

"I'm heading home. I'm exhausted, Ryan. Thank you again for all that you did and have done for me. It truly is appreciated."

"I'll take you home."

"No, that's okay. I'm going to call a cab."

"Don't be silly, I can take you."

She looked at him for a moment. He had been everything that she needed over the past week. But she couldn't allow him to get closer. She knew she'd never win his heart. He had said it. He had stated he was fine being on his own. She needed now to distance herself from him.

"Ryan. I'll return your things to you this week. I'm going to go home now by cab. You stay here and spend time with your parents and these other fine people. I'm tired, I don't want to argue with you so just let me go. I'll be fine. I need to be alone."

"I'm only trying to help you," he said in frustration.

"I know and thank you. You've done enough. It's time for me to pull up my big girl panties and take care of things from here on in. Again, I appreciate what you've done. Good night, Ryan. I've already said goodbye to your parents. Take care." She turned and walked out onto the porch of Giovanni's, closing the door behind her, and called a cab.

Ryan stood there, staring at the closed door, trying to comprehend what just happened. She had been almost cold towards him at a time when he needed her warmth. He could feel his body tremble, and he rubbed his right temple where a headache was starting to set in.

"You okay, son?" his father asked as he approached the front door.

"Uh, no Dad, I don't think I am." He explained what had happened and how ridiculous it all seemed.

"She's in love with you," Jeff stated.

"Clearly not," Ryan argued in frustration.

"Don't give up but give her a bit of space. It's five o'clock. Do you want to grab some dinner?"

"Thanks, but I'll pass."

"Your mom and I are going to drive home. We'll see you Christmas day. You call me if there's anything you need."

Ann came to the door, put on her coat, kissed her son, and said goodbye. "You take care of that girl. She loves you." She stepped out the door with Jeff and closed it behind them.

One by one the people left and by six-thirty, Giovanni's was empty, with the exception of the wait staff, kitchen staff, Lorenzo, and Ryan.

"Thank you, man, for doing all of this for Emma. I hope what I gave you was enough to cover the food, drinks, and lost revenue from closing."

"It's all good. I'm glad you made this happen for her. When did she leave? And more importantly, why didn't you take her home?"

"Oh, I wanted to, but she insisted on going by cab. She told me that I've done enough for her and she was going to, how did she put it, 'pull up her big girl panties and deal with things on her own' now."

"Ouch."

"Yeah, ouch. But I'll give her time. She needs time. She stayed because she thought she would have two to three weeks with her mom. She had five days. That, in itself, must be devastating for her."

"I agree. Give her a bit of space. She loves you, you know."

"Why does everyone keep saying that? She clearly doesn't. She told me she doesn't need me anymore."

"Oh, but she does. She doesn't need you to help her anymore. The worst is over. She needs more from you."

Ryan dropped his head. "I don't know if I can give her what she wants. I talked to Cathy the other night about it. Cathy wants me to move on and be happy but as much as I want to, I'd still feel like I was betraying her. I'm so torn."

"Ryan, she's been gone eight years. How long are you going to wait to be happy? And, will another chance like Emma come around again? Think about that."

Lorenzo got up and went to the bar. He filled two glasses with his best brandy and carried them back to the table. "Here, drink this and then go home and get some rest. It's been quite a day for you, too. I see how much it takes from you to see Emma suffer. Call her in a couple of days. I'm sure she will be happy to hear from you."

"Thanks, I'll talk with you soon." Ryan finished his drink and left for home.

Chapter 12

It was less than a week until Christmas and Emma, lost now without her mom, immersed herself in her painting. She had spent the day following the funeral, moving furniture from the office, into her mother's bedroom. She put down plastic sheeting over the carpet, tarps on top of that, and then a fabric painter's cloth over that so that there was no chance of ruining the carpet. She set up her portable easel which she had ordered online with canvases and had them delivered to what was now her home. Something she would have to get used to saying and meaning.

Emma's phone rang regularly throughout the day, mainly people checking on her to see how she was fairing. Only after checking to see who it was, did she decide whether she should take the call or not. When Julie called, she answered, giving her the usual update of being fine and just needing time, and Julie was accepting of that.

When Ryan called, she let the call go to voice mail. He had left several messages already, and she'd not listened to any.

Her heart had been shattered and living in the house amongst her mother's things was a constant reminder of how she had failed her mom. She wasn't the daughter that she should have been. The guilt coursed through her, and she felt alone with hard decisions that had to be made.

Should she live in the small town, work in the store, paint, and live in her mom's house? Or should she go back to the city where she was more alone. If she stayed, she would at least have the company of Julie and Katie, and she was sure she would have a better chance of making more friends here. There didn't seem to be much hope of that in the city as she would just fall back into the routine she'd had for the last ten years: work, home, sleep, and do it again the next day.

Her head hurt while she contemplated all that still needed to be done. Sooner rather than later would be best. What better way to escape the world, and the pain, than in her paintings? Emma walked into the office with a bottle of wine and a glass, filled the glass, and sat on the stool in front of the canvas. Closing her eyes, she let the vision of the canvas coming to life, settle in her head. She took her time, making sure she saw all of the details. And when she opened her eyes and picked up the brush, she was ready to let it flow out of her.

She squeezed the tubes of colors onto her palette and dipped her brush into them, one by one, mixing to the desired hue. The brush flowed over the canvas with a purpose and when she was done, six hours later, so was the wine.

Sitting back further on the stool, Emma closed her eyes to envision what she had seen before. When she opened her eyes, she saw the same image on her canvas. It was a beautiful portrait of her mother, full of life as she had been before getting sick.

Emma cried. She missed her mom dearly.

The doorbell rang, interrupting Emma's thoughts, and she went to answer it.

"Ryan, what are you doing here?"

"I'm worried about you. You're not taking my calls, you're not returning my calls after I leave a message. I needed to know that you were okay."

"I'm fine, thank you. I just need some time and space."

He saw the smock on her and knew she had been painting, and crying, by the looks of her eyes and face, and he guessed that she had also been drinking. "Emma, it's not good for you to be alone. Let me stay with you for a bit."

"Would you like some wine?" she asked as she turned to go into the kitchen.

He stepped through the door and removed his jacket and boots. "Sure."

"I just need to run upstairs and get my glass. I'll be right down," she said after pulling the bottle from the fridge. "Why don't you open this in the meantime?"

Ryan watched as she half stumbled up the stairs and when she didn't come back down after five minutes, he went up to see what was wrong.

Sitting on her stool in front of the painting, Emma shed silent tears, looking at her mom once more.

"Oh, Emma, she's beautiful," he said, moving up behind her. He put his hands on her shoulders and gave them a light squeeze. "You did an amazing likeness of her. It feels like she's right here."

"I miss her so much," she cried.

He scooped her up off the stool and hugged her. "I know you do. I know it's hard. It will get easier as time goes on. You won't forget her, it just gets a little easier to move through your days without her as time goes on."

She cried into his shoulder for a while longer. "I don't know what to do anymore."

"She's here with you, Emma. She's here. You've captured her essence in your painting and that came from your heart."

"Yes, but I don't know what to do," she said looking up at him.

"What do you mean?"

"I have some decisions to make and I don't know what to do."

"Tell you what. Go freshen up, come downstairs, I'll light a fire and we can talk about it."

She didn't move. She didn't take her eyes off him. He could sense what she was thinking as the desire burned in him as well. But he wasn't about to confuse her more. He stepped back, turned her to the door, and walked with her to the bathroom. "Put some water on your face, you'll feel better, and then come down and have some wine."

When she stepped into the bathroom, she understood why he showed no interest in kissing her. Her face was a mess… blackened by the mascara running under her eyes, her hair was disheveled, and she looked pale. She did her best to clean herself up.

Ryan, in the meantime, retrieved the wine glass and the empty bottle from the office, stopping once more to admire the portrait of Susan, and then went down to the kitchen. He picked up the bottle that had been pulled from the fridge and refilled her glass. He pulled another glass from the cupboard, filling that as well. He carried them into the family room and set them on the table. He lit a fire, dimmed the lights, and waited for her.

She arrived a few minutes later, looking better than she had before. "Thank you. I'm always thanking you."

"There's no need to thank me for anything, Emma. I'm happy to help you with whatever you need. Now come, sit down and tell me what's bothering you."

She sat next to him across from the fireplace. She felt the warmth of it and the heat from him. "I need to decide where I want to be," she said. "Mom has left the house and the store to me. I can't figure out if I want to stay here or if I want to go back to life in the city."

"Well, let's break it down. What would be keeping you in the city?"

"My job."

He waited for more but when that didn't happen he spoke up. "That's it? Your job?"

"I make good money doing what I'm doing. I enjoy the benefits of a good income."

He smiled. "And what would you do with all your money?"

"I'd buy a house."

"And where would you buy your house?"

"In the country, I love the countryside."

"You have a house in the country."

"But I don't have a job in the country."

"You own a store."

"Ughhh. Yes, I know but I won't make the kind of money that I'm making now."

"How much more money do you need?" he asked smiling inwardly.

"I don't know. Enough to pay off the house."

"You don't think this house is paid off?"

"Yes, I'm sure it is."

"Then what do you need that kind of money for?"

"I don't know.....maybe to buy paint supplies, clothes, you know." She sipped her wine.

"Emma. Would you be leaving a lot of friends behind?"

"No," she replied, feeling embarrassed.

"You have no friends?" he asked jokingly.

"Hey, I have friends, we just don't see each other that much."

"Okay, well you could make new friends here. Julie is your friend, Katie would be a friend. Lorenzo is your friend. I'm your friend, and you've only been here just over a week. See how quickly that works?" he laughed. "Just think, if you made 4 new friends every week, in a year, you'd have too many friends to keep track of."

She couldn't help but laugh with him. It felt good to laugh. It was the first time in a long time that she had done that. And then the guilt of laughing took over. She should be doing that. She was mourning her mother's death.

"Emma, seriously, think about staying here." He turned her face in his direction and looked into her eyes. "I'd love to get to know you better. There's something about you that I can't let go of."

When she didn't say anything and kept her eyes locked with his, he pulled her in for a kiss, and the moment she realized what was happening, she pulled back.

"Ryan," she said. "I don't want to start something that can't be finished. I don't know if I'm staying and you've already stated that you're just fine on your own. Why start something now." She got up from the sofa and moved to the fire, to get away from the heat of him. She could easily fall for this man, but she didn't want to be completely crushed if he broke her heart.

Knowing that this wasn't the time to push things with her, he changed the subject. "Okay, then let's be friends. When was the last time you ate something?"

"I'm not sure. I don't remember."

"Then let's get some food into you. Why don't we go get a pizza or would you rather order in?"

"I'm really not that hungry."

"You have to eat, Emma. Otherwise you are going to get sick and I'm not about to let that happen. We can order in, watch a movie, and then I'll go so that you can get some sleep. How does that sound?"

"All right."

"Does your mom have Netflix?"

"I don't know."

"Let's see if she does." He turned on the TV, used the remote to move from one screen to another, and found that she did indeed. "Great, we just need to decide what to watch. Why don't you scroll through the listings and see if there is anything you'd like to see. I'll order pizza. What do you want on the pizza?"

"I'm fine with anything as long as there are no anchovies or pineapple on it. And nothing too spicy."

"Perfect."

As she scrolled through the listings, he placed the order and then sat with her hoping she'd find something she liked. He didn't care what they watched, he just enjoyed being with her.

By the time the pizza arrived, they had chosen the movie and Emma got plates and napkins from the kitchen. Ryan watched as she moved from one room to the other, admiring her slim figure and how it moved. Her medium length brown hair, messy as it was, suited her perfectly, he wished he could run his fingers through it.

They opened the pizza box to a fresh, hot, pepperoni pizza with tomatoes, green peppers, onion, and extra cheese. Each pulled two slices onto their plates and then sat back for the movie.

The romantic thriller that she chose had her sitting on the edge of her seat, and he enjoyed watching her reactions. She got right into it, covering her eyes when the plot thickened, laughing at the funny spots, and crying when something awful happened. When it was done, she looked at him as if she had been in the movie, going through the events herself. He laughed.

"What are you laughing at?"

"I've never seen anyone get into a movie like that before."

"It was a great movie."

"Yes, it was, but I enjoyed watching you watch it more." He pulled her over and hugged her. "I'm glad you enjoyed it."

She quickly got up and moved the plates and pizza to the kitchen, to avoid falling into the embrace and losing herself in it. He felt the uneasiness she had and let her go.

"Emma, would you like to go to the tree lighting on Saturday with me?" He got up and went to her.

"I don't feel like doing Christmas anymore."

"The first Christmas without them is the hardest. Let me help you make it a little easier. I won't be able to be here on Christmas Day as I've promised to be home, so let's spend Christmas Eve together."

"I'll think about it, Ryan. I can't make any promises."

"I can't ask for more than that. Now, I'll go home as promised so that you can get some sleep," he said, walking to the front door. "Emma, please don't hesitate to call me if there's anything I can do for you. Even if it's just to talk, I'm here for you."

She followed him to the door. "Thank you, Ryan, would you like the rest of the pizza?"

"No, you keep it. Eat. You're going to waste away to nothing," he smiled.

"I'll be fine."

"Emma, think about what I said about staying. You have friends here. You'll discover what your parents loved about this small town. You could get a good job here, too, if you didn't want to keep the store and earn enough for your day-to-day needs. You have a house that's paid off and if you decide to keep the store and have people run it for you, you'd have earnings from that as well. That can all be worked out. Think about it, please. I think you'll come to love this small town as I do."

"I have an appointment with the lawyer tomorrow. Then I'll decide. But, yes, I'll think about it. Thank you for the company tonight. It helped." She stepped towards him to hug him, knowing how difficult it was going to be to step away from him again.

The embrace lasted longer than it should have, each taking what they needed from it in the moment, and then Emma stepped back.

"Good night, Ryan," she said, with a quiver in her voice.

"Night, Emma." He pulled the door open and stepped out. "I enjoyed my time with you."

She closed the door, turned off the hall light, and sat in the family room once more. She thought about what he had said. Staying. It did appeal to her. He appealed to her, and she wished that she could explore that more, but she wasn't sure if her heart could take another beating. Was it better to move back to the city, she wondered. Out of sight, out of mind, right?

She pulled out her phone and set up a reminder for the next day to check the classifieds and job opportunities through agencies, if they had any in the small town.

Did she want to go to the tree lighting? Had it not been this difficult time, she might enjoy it. A small-town Christmas was something to be experienced.

She remembered her mom asking her to do something for the community. She wondered what she could do. She entered another reminder into the phone to check that out. She needed to speak to the lawyer first, check the bank accounts, and then decide what the community might need the most.

Emma shut down the fire, put away her wine glass, and bottle, and went to bed.

Ryan lay on his bed in just his boxers, thinking about the evening. He thought he may have made a little progress, but sometimes Emma seemed hard to read. On the one hand, he could feel her pushing him away, and in the next moment, he felt like she was looking for more. Mixed signals. He hated mixed signals. If he pushed for more, he may be pushing her away.

He thought back on how she lived in the moment with the movie as if she were playing the role of the main character. How he loved watching the emotions cross her face and couldn't help but feel the attraction to that. Something he never expected.

And the painting. He was amazed at her talent. The talent she didn't know she had. She could make a lot of money just with her paintings. Something he could mention the next time that subject came up. How innocent she was in some ways. He tossed and turned for most of the night, thinking about her and eventually fell asleep.

Chapter 13

Emma was up early to prepare herself for the meeting with the lawyer. She knew what the lawyer would tell her as her mother had told her that she was the sole beneficiary. But it was something that needed to be done.

Upon arrival, she was ushered into the office of C. Stanfield and was pleasantly surprised to see a woman about her age. She was tall, slim, and dressed in a business suit. Her brown skin glowed from the light that came through the window next to her mahogany desk. Her dark hair ran straight down the side of her face, touching her shoulders. She smiled as Emma entered.

"Good morning, Emmalee Jones. Please, come in and make yourself comfortable," she said, walking around the desk to shake Emma's hand. "I'm Cathy Stanfield."

"Good morning. Thank you, Cathy. Please, call me Emma." Emma sat in the chair across from the desk and nervously smoothed her skirt over her knees.

"I'm so sorry to hear about your mom. My sincerest condolences," she said going back to her own chair. When she sat, she pulled a file from the corner of her desk. "Is there anything I can get you? Coffee? Tea perhaps?"

"Coffee would be lovely, thank you."

Cathy called to her assistant, asking for coffee. "Your mother and I spent a bit of time together. She was a beautiful soul. I knew your father also, but not as well as your mother. I wasn't handling anything at that point for your parents. When Rob Cleary died, I took over his clients. Your parents were his clients but your father passed away shortly after our first meeting."

Emma twisted the end of the red silk scarf she was wearing. She could feel her emotions rising and was afraid she'd fall apart.

The assistant came in with a tray holding two mugs of coffee, cream, and sugar, and she placed it on the corner of the big desk.

"Help yourself," Cathy said.

Emma fixed her coffee, as Cathy opened the folder and continued. "Your mom came in to see me about two months ago. She told me about her cancer and asked that I make a few changes to the original will. As you are the sole beneficiary, you will be the only one here today for the reading. So, let's get that out of the way."

Emma sat back with her coffee mug, preparing herself for more. Cathy quickly added a bit of sugar to the mug that was on the tray and proceeded to read the will to Emma. The will stated everything that Susan had told Emma. The home was paid off and Emma was to inherit that, the business was being handed over, the money in the bank accounts was all hers, but there was a surprise at the end.

"Now, this is where the change came when she visited with me a couple of weeks ago. A note to you and I have an envelope in my safe for you. Shall I read it or would you like to read it yourself?"

"As you already know what it says, please feel free to read it. I don't think I'd be able to hold the page still enough to read it," Emma responded.

"Alright, it says, 'Dearest Emmie, I have left this envelope with Cathy Stanfield for you. In it, you will find a winning ticket to the lottery. I have no use for the money at this point anymore so it's yours. I hope this will bring you an easier life so you don't have to work so hard. I'm hoping you will stay in the house and get to know the wonderful people in this community. Your father and I loved it here in Willowbrook and I think you will too if you give it a chance. The ticket should help you with the move and get you settled here. Your father and I have always been so proud of you. You're the best daughter anyone could ask for. We'll be watching over you from Heaven and know that we love you always. Love, Mom.'"

Cathy got up from her chair and went to her safe. She pulled out the envelope and handed it to Emma. "Susan never told me how much the ticket was worth but said that there was a note inside so that you could see. The envelope is sealed, as you can see, and it hasn't been opened."

With tears running down Emma's face, and hands shaking uncontrollably, she slowly opened the envelope. She pulled out the ticket and the note that was with it. After reading the note, she looked up at Cathy with gaping eyes. "I….I don't know what to do with this," she stammered. Her hands shook so badly it was difficult for her to hang onto the ticket so she returned it to the envelope and placed it on the desk.

"Is it something you'd like to talk about?" Cathy asked. "I'm here to help you with anything you need. I'm guessing that since it was a ticket and she gave it to me to keep for you, it must be a larger sum of money. I can advise you on how to proceed with it."

"I need to think, please give me a minute," Emma said.

"Absolutely, take your time. I don't have another appointment today until mid-afternoon. We have a few hours."

Emma sipped at her coffee, wondering what she should do. Can she trust this woman? It came to her, shortly after. *Mom had enough trust in you, why wouldn't I?*

"According to the note mom has with this, the ticket is worth a million dollars. It's one of the guaranteed million dollar prizes for that draw."

"Well, congratulations! How wonderful for you," Cathy stated in delight.

"It's too bad that my mother couldn't enjoy the benefit of it," Emma cried.

Cathy pulled the tissue box from the wall unit behind her and passed it to Emma who gratefully pulled a couple of tissues and wiped her eyes and nose.

"Thank you."

"So, let's talk about the steps that you might want to take with everything," Cathy said, once she knew Emma was ready to continue.

For the next two hours, they talked about what needed to be done, not only with the ticket, but the steps to be taken with the business, the bank, and the house. When they finished with that, they both enjoyed another cup of coffee together and talked about other things, building a friendship.

"You've been a huge help to me today," Emma said. "I'd like to keep you as my lawyer going forward."

"Does that mean you've decided to stay in our wonderful small town?"

"Yes, I think I'm going to give it a go. I think I'll head home this afternoon, get things packed up, arrange a truck, and speak to my Real Estate agent, Marcus Herley, about selling the condo. I should be back by the weekend."

"Sounds great."

"I'd like you to do something for me though," Emma gave Cathy some instructions and when she was done, she felt much better and was now on a mission.

She knew now what she wanted and what she had to do to accomplish that.

"Thank you so much for all your help. I didn't mean to take up so much of your time," Emma said to Cathy.

"My pleasure. We should get together for coffee sometime, on a more personal level. I enjoyed talking to you. Call me when you have time."

"I'll do that. Thank you."

When she left the lawyer's office, she felt like she made a new friend. She called Julie. "Hi Julie, how are you?"

"I'm doing fine dear, how are you doing is the question?" she asked.

"I'm doing a bit better. I just wanted you to know that I'm heading home this afternoon. But I will be back at some point.

There are things that need to be taken care of. I wanted to let you know so that you don't worry."

"You're not staying?"

"I need to go home. I'll keep in touch with you. Would you please call Ryan to let him know? I'm super busy and need to get on the road now if I'm going to make it back to the city at a decent hour."

"All right dear, you get home safe. Please keep in touch."

"I will. Thank you for all that you have done. I'll talk with you soon."

Emma rushed home, packed a couple of things, and drove to Giftable You. When she got there, she saw a young lady at the cash register and approached her. "Hi, is Katie here?"

"No, she had to step out for a couple of minutes, can I help you?"

"No, that's all right. Please let her know that Emma stopped in and I'll call her later."

"I'll do that. Have a good day."

Emma climbed back into her car and drove to the city. On her drive, she called Marcus Herley about the sale of the condo and arranged to drop in the next day to get things rolling. From there, it was an enjoyable drive back, knowing that she was packing up her life for a better one. The decision that she made felt right, and now she was at ease with it.

Emma arrived at her condo building at seven that evening. As she stepped out of the car, her phone fell out of her purse and dropped to the concrete, shattering the glass. She quickly picked it up and tested it to see if it worked. It didn't. She took her things to her condo and sat on the sofa to try and fix it but to no avail.

I'll buy a new one in the morning.

It was getting late in the day, and she was tired from the drive. The morning would be soon enough. There was much to do the next day.

Giving up on the phone, she went into her bedroom and pulled everything from the drawers of her dresser, making neat piles on the bedroom floor. She opened her closet and pulled out anything that wasn't hanging and did the same. She removed the pictures from the walls and collected all the items from her nightstand and from the top of her dresser, placing them on the floor. She wanted to get a feel for how many boxes she would require for the move.

She cleaned out her bathroom and hall closets, much the same way and when she approached the kitchen and opened the cupboards, she realized that this was a bigger job than she first thought. She was tired and would tackle it the next day.

Emma worked on a list of what needed to be done for the next two days. First thing in the morning, she would visit the lottery office with her ticket that her mom left to her and claim the prize. Cathy had made sure that she signed the ticket before she left the office.

Then she would buy a new phone and get all her information transferred from the old phone to the new one if that were possible.

She would then call movers, book the truck for Friday morning, and ask if they had boxes that she could purchase. It would save her considerable time. She knew she'd have to pack quickly, but she wasn't too concerned about getting it done. She wasn't a hoarder, she was quite the opposite, purging unneeded things on a regular basis. She loved clean, open spaces.

Then she would drop into her office, explain her situation and give her notice. She would work from her new home if needed.

She would drop in and see Marcus and get papers signed for the sale of the condo.

Then, she'd pick up boxes and pack as much as possible before movers arrived the next day. It promised to be a hectic day.

She sat on the sofa, double-checking her list when the day's events took its toll on her and the tiredness crept in. Taking a moment to reflect on the last two weeks, she closed her eyes and felt the presence of her mom and dad, smiling over her in approval, and was reassured, in that moment, that she was doing the right thing.

She got herself ready for bed, and as soon as her head hit the pillow, she fell asleep.

Ryan called Emma numerous times that same afternoon, and it went straight to voice mail. He left several messages, but none were returned. When he got home, he noticed that her car was no longer in the driveway. Maybe she put it into the garage, he thought, and went over to knock on the door. When there was no answer, he walked home again. He checked throughout the evening to see if there were any lights on and there weren't. Before going to bed that night, he checked once more.

He wondered where she might have gone as she was still new to the area, and he didn't think that she had made any friends yet except Julie and Katie. He'd call Julie in the morning, he thought, and went to bed, but he spent the night tossing and turning. He was worried. What if something had happened to her?

Unable to sleep, Ryan got up at four o'clock in the morning and felt sick to his stomach. The worry that she had caused him was unforgivable. He tried calling again, and once more it went to voice mail. "Why doesn't she answer?" he snapped. This time, he didn't leave a message.

He paced around the house for the next three hours, until he thought it was a decent enough hour to make calls. Julie was the first on the list.

"Good morning, Julie. Have you heard from Emma? I'm worried sick about her. She's not answering my calls."

"Good morning, Ryan. I'm so sorry. I was supposed to call you yesterday. I forgot."

"Why were you supposed to call me?"

"Julie went home yesterday. She told me to let you know. She said she would be back at some point because there were things to take care of, but she's in the city now."

A wave of disappointment washed over Ryan. He was speechless for a moment.

"Thank you, Julie. I'll talk with you soon," and he disconnected the call.

Now he knew, he thought. She didn't want him in her life. If she did, she would have called him.

Ryan's heart broke. He took extra time before going into work, resigning himself that she didn't need him after all. He made a pot of coffee and let the emotions wash through him so that he could move on with his life. He sipped at his coffee as he thought about all that had happened over the past almost two weeks.

He berated himself for letting himself fall for her so quickly. "Never again," he mumbled. "Who needs women?"

When he felt ready, he went to work but found, after an hour, that he couldn't focus on anything. He told his staff that he'd be out for the rest of the day and left.

"Lorenzo, where are you?" he asked when he placed the call to his friend as he was leaving his office.

"At the restaurant, why?"

"Can I swing by?"

"Sure, I'm just doing some paperwork. See you in a bit."

When Ryan reached the restaurant, he rang the bell as the door was still locked. Lorenzo answered it immediately. "Hey, you look like crap. What's going on?" he asked.

"She left," he grumbled.

"Who left?"

"Emma. She left. Didn't say goodbye, not a word, just left."

"What? She went home?"

"Yeah. No goodbye, nothing."

"What did you do to her?" Lorenzo asked as he led Ryan back to the bar.

"What do you mean 'what did you do to her'? I was nice to her."

"Come on, I know you. You said something that you shouldn't have."

"I swear, I was nice to her. I was over at her place Tuesday night. We had pizza, watched a movie, and all was good before I left that night."

"So, what happened?"

"I - don't - know," he stressed. "I tried calling yesterday afternoon and there was no answer. I called a few times. Even left messages but she never returned my call."

"She was busy. Obviously."

"Yeah, busy leaving. I swear I got home after work yesterday, the car was gone. I thought, she was out shopping. I waited, checked constantly. I started to get worried but there was nothing I could do. I felt helpless. I was up most of the night worrying."

"Sure looks like that." Lorenzo snickered.

Ryan gave Lorenzo a look that let him know he wasn't amused.

"Aw, I'm sorry. Here, have a drink." He poured Ryan a scotch on the rocks and one for himself.

"I'm done with women. I can't handle the heartbreaks."

"She loves you, you know?"

"Yeah, right. That's why she left."

"I saw it in the way she looked at you. Both times she was here. She does love you."

"She sure has a funny way of showing it."

"Look, hear me out. There are always two people in a relationship and right now, all I hear is you. She's been through a lot in the past two weeks, you need to give her time and space to grieve and to figure out what she wants. Do you know what she wants? Probably not. Why? I don't know. Maybe because she doesn't know what she wants. Maybe she's gone home to figure that out. Give her space, man. If it's meant to be, she'll be back."

"I didn't know one could fall in love so quickly," Ryan said softly. "I would have laughed at you had you told me that you loved someone after just two weeks. It's insane. I haven't even kissed her yet."

"Ah, and there you have it."

"What?"

"You haven't kissed her. Maybe she thinks you aren't interested."

"Oh, I've wanted to, but she always seemed so fragile and it never seemed to be the right time. Came close once but we were interrupted. I haven't tried since because I didn't want to take advantage of her vulnerability as I do realize she's going through a lot. See, I am understanding."

"She'll be back. Give her time. I'll put a wager on it." Lorenzo reassured.

"Okay, put your money where your mouth is. I should at least get something out of this."

"Twenty bucks says she's back before Christmas."

"You're on," Ryan said putting out his hand, and they shook on it.

"Now, go home and forget about it for now. She's a grown woman who can take care of herself. She's done it for years without you."

Ryan finished his drink and thanked his friend. When he got home, he napped on the sofa while the TV offered the day's news.

Emma's day had gone much as planned. She had visited the lottery offices where she claimed her prize. She then purchased a new phone and left her broken phone with the technician in the store to see if they could retrieve data from it to the new phone.

She stopped into her office and spoke to her boss, explaining her situation, and they discussed her exit from the company with their best wishes. Nisha would be moved into her position and Emma would be available to help if needed. She spoke with Nisha briefly to update her about her plans.

"I'm thrilled that you are doing something that will make you happy, Emma. And I think Ryan will be good for you," Nisha said.

"What do you mean, Ryan will be good for me? How does he have anything to do with this?"

"Oh, come on now. Aren't you moving to be near him?"

"No," Emma stressed. "I'm moving because I like it there. I love the small-town feel, the people, and I have a business there. It has nothing to do with Ryan."

"Uh-huh. So you say. I saw how he looks at you and how you look at him. There's a definite love vibe going on there."

"You're imagining things. He's a friend. He helped me out a lot. Supported me in every way that I needed while Mom was dying. But that's it."

"Uh-huh."

"Really, there's nothing there and there won't be. He told me he had no intentions of getting involved with anyone because he's fine being on his own."

"Uh-huh."

"Oh, your incorrigible." she stated out of frustration.

"Look, you believe what you want to, but I know, and trust me, he's interested. Enough said."

"Right. Well, I have a very busy day. I have to be packed by the end of the day."

"Need help?"

"I should be fine but if you want, come over, we can have a drink before I leave. I also hope you come up and visit me when I'm settled. It will be nice in the summer. There's a beach nearby."

"Sounds like a plan. I'll swing by after work to see if you still need help. Now go, let me get back to work, and you pack, girl."

Emma went to her desk, gathered up her personal belongings, hugged her friend, and left. She felt at ease about the choice she made and was leaving in good standings. She had remembered her father telling her to never burn bridges because you never know if you need to cross them again. She knew she didn't burn this bridge.

Returning to the store where she purchased her phone and was pleased to find out that they had been successful in transferring data.

She then stopped in to see Marcus about the sale of her condo. "Thank you for taking care of this so quickly," she said as she walked towards him. " If you could arrange a cleaning crew to go in and clean up what's needed to make a good sale, get a stager in, that would be great."

"That shouldn't be a problem," Marcus replied. "I have people that can do all that for you."

"Great, I can drop the key off on Friday after the movers are loaded. If you wouldn't mind arranging for the remaining furniture to go to a charitable organization or wherever you feel would benefit from it, I'd appreciate it. I'll take care of all the expenses of course." He assured her that all would be taken care of.

Calling for movers was a challenge as it would need to be an emergency move for Friday morning. It was super short notice and her plan almost fell apart because of it. She had called eight reputable moving companies before finding one that had just had a cancellation. They told her they could pack up her things into a container but they couldn't actually do the move until the following Wednesday as they didn't have the extra eight hours to spare. She could have the full day on Wednesday, if that was agreeable with her. She agreed, knowing that with such short notice she wasn't going to get anything better, especially with the Christmas holidays falling in-between. She asked if they had boxes that she could purchase, which they did, and went to pick them up along with other packing supplies.

When she got back to her condo at two o'clock to begin the packing process, she enlisted the help of the security guard to bring up all the boxes and packing supplies to her condo. Emma poured a glass of orange juice for herself sat for a moment to catch her breath before beginning the packing process.

Emma taped the box bottoms and filled them with the items she had laid out the night before. She had fourteen boxes done when a call came up from the lobby announcing Nisha's arrival. She needed a break at that point and was happy when Nisha stepped through the door.

"Look at you," Nisha exclaimed. "You've done so much already. How can I help."

"I need a break, you can have a drink with me and let me just rest for a few minutes. Then you can help me fill these boxes." Emma went into the kitchen and came back with two wine glasses and a bottle of wine. Once the wine was poured, they chatted about work and her life up north.

"So you're going to run your mom's store now?" Nisha asked.

Emma hesitated for a moment wondering if she should tell her friend of her mother's ticket. She didn't want a lot of people to know. "Um, actually no. I'm handing the store over to my mother's friend who has been running it for the last year on her own. She deserves it. I really don't have an interest in it but don't tell Mr. Evans. I told him I was taking it over."

"Why would you lie?" Nisha asked.

"Only because I'm not completely sure what I'm going to be doing there. It was just easy to use that."

"I get it. So, what were you thinking about doing? You need to be able to support yourself somehow."

"Agreed. But the house is paid off and I'll only need money for the upkeep, taxes, and my groceries and personal things. That's not much."

"But it's still something. You need a job."

"I'm going to take my time. Mom left me some money. I have enough to get by for a while." Emma sipped her wine, thinking of her mom again and could feel the emotions start to take over again. "I need to get busy again before I sit here and blubber once more."

"You're going to have those moments for a long time yet. Use them, it's perfectly natural to grieve for a while. It's all still fresh."

Emma wiped tears from her eyes with the sleeve of her sweater. "Well, I'll take that time later when everything is done. I've got movers coming first thing in the morning and need to get this done."

"How can I help?"

Emma gave Nisha instructions on what to do. Three hours later, only stopping once for the pizza that arrived, all the boxes had been packed, the paintings had been bubble wrapped and strapped together in lots of two or three. The TV had been disconnected and taken down and wrapped in bubble wrap. All other electronics had been disconnected and packed. Kitchen cupboards were bare and the only thing left was the bedding on her bed and toiletries that she would still need which she would take back with her. They looked through all the cupboards and closets to make sure all had been packed.

"Well, that went quicker than I thought it would. Thank you so much for your help. Do you want another glass of wine?"

"No, I need to get home. Tomorrow's a workday for me. You didn't have that much stuff, that's why it went quickly."

"Yes, I know. I purge constantly." Emma walked with Nisha to the door. "Keep in touch, okay? I'm going to miss you."

"I'll miss you, too. Thanks for the pizza and the wine." she replied before hugging Emma, and leaving.

Emma pushed her hair back from her face as she looked around to see what remained to be done. She had left the curtains so that the condo could be staged properly for sale. The white sheers let in a lot of light during the day and that would help. She wasn't sure she needed them in the house.

She had thought about Ryan often throughout the day and had wanted to call, but she was caught up in the move that it slipped her mind. Her body ached, and she was tired, she decided to surprise him the next day. She finished her glass of wine and went to bed. As soon as her head hit the pillow, she fell into a deep sleep.

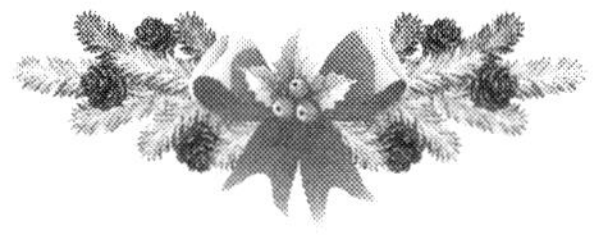

Chapter 14

It was still dark when Emma awoke on Friday morning, and the alarm clock by her bed had not gone off. She briefly pondered how her life would be and whether she was making the best choices for herself. Was she truly going to be happy?

She got out of bed, feeling the ache all over her body, and stepped into a hot shower, thinking that the heat would help her muscles relax. She put on the jeans and blue sweater she'd left on the chair and set about packing the bedding into the last box, sealing and marking it, and placing the toiletries she didn't need into a bag she'd take with her.

The movers were scheduled to arrive at 8:00 a.m., giving her an hour to finish some last-minute tasks. She rinsed the wine glasses from the day before, wrapped them, and placed them in the kitchen's last open box. Emma gathered the trash and carried it down the hall to the garbage chute and put red labels on the backs of a few objects to indicate that she wanted them shipped to her once the condo was sold. She wrote

Marcus a note with a list of the items that had the stickers on them and took a picture of that list with her new phone.

When the movers arrived, she was prepared and watched as they emptied her condo of all the numbered boxes, paintings, and bags that she had filled. By eleven o'clock, they were finished. She conducted another quick walk-through to make sure everything that was intended to go did, and when she was satisfied, she picked up her personal things and left the condo for the last time, locking the door behind her.

Emma was apprehensive since it had just begun to snow, and she wondered what the weather would be like on the drive north. She despised driving in the snow. It wasn't so much about her driving that made her nervous, but the odd idiot that tended to be around her wherever she drove. She knew she was a good driver, taking her time and watching her speed.

Emma traveled across town to give Marcus the key and instructed him to send any paperwork to her via email. She double-checked that he had the right one.

She drove north on the highway after picking up a large coffee from a Tim Horton's drive-through, and was able to relax more once she was out of the city because there was little traffic. She cranked up the music and sat back in the car, eager to go home and surprise Ryan.

Emma pulled into the driveway of her Willowbrook home three hours later. She parked her car next to her mother's in the double garage, knowing she wouldn't need it for a while. She had stopped in town to get some groceries before heading home, and she knew she could stroll into town if she needed anything else. She didn't have any plans to do so though. She'd heard it was going to start snowing on Saturday, and she reasoned that leaving the driveway empty would make shoveling easier.

She carried her belongings and groceries into the house, unpacked, and settled into the family room. All she wanted was a quiet evening as exhaustion finally overpowered her. She sat in front of the TV to watch a movie but soon fell asleep. At 7:00 p.m., she awoke to a dark house and chastised herself for falling asleep. She was still exhausted, too exhausted to visit Ryan. She resolved to call him first thing in the morning.

Her phone rang a few minutes later. Seeing it was Julie, she answered.

"Hi, Julie, how are you?"

"I'm doing just fine. I just wanted to check on you. I've been worried. Is everything okay?"

"Julie, I'm fine and I'm back. I'm back to stay."

"That's wonderful, dear! I'm so glad to hear that. Listen, it's Christmas on Sunday. Would you like to come over for Christmas dinner? I don't like the thought of you being alone."

"Aw, that's such a kind offer, but if you don't mind, I'd like to spend Christmas by myself. I don't think I'll make good company as it will be the first Christmas without Mom. But thank you for the offer."

"Well, if you change your mind, you know where I am. I'll have plenty of food to go around and you are always welcome here."

"Thank you, Julie. We can have a coffee or tea together in the next few days. I need to get myself organized a bit better, then I'll call."

"Whenever you are ready. Call me if you need anything."

"Will do. Have a good night."

"You, too."

Emma went to the kitchen and fixed herself some dinner, poured a glass of wine, and watched a movie on Netflix, making notes in her phone of things she wanted to do as they came to her through the movie. Selling her mom's car was one of those things.

A little past nine o'clock, Emma heard a soft knocking at the door. When she went to answer it, she was surprised to see

Ryan standing there. He seemed just as surprised that she answered the door.

"Hi, come in," she said, flipping on the hall light.

"No, that's all right. Your house has been dark the last couple of days. I saw an extra light on today and just thought I'd check it out since your car wasn't in the driveway."

"Well, that's good of you to do that. Come in, get out of the cold."

He stepped in and she closed the door. "How have you been?" she asked, noting that he looked a little ragged. He had worry lines on his forehead and his eyes looked dark and sad. His face looked thin and unshaven.

"Fine. I'm doing just fine. Everything okay here?"

"Yes, all is fine." There was an awkward pause where neither knew what to say.

Ryan flashed her a worried look. She appeared very tired, and he wondered if she had gotten any sleep. But he couldn't do anything about it. "All right," Ryan said, breaking the silence. "It's good to know that everything is all right. I'm going home. You have a good night." He shifted his weight to open the door.

"Ryan, what's going on?"

He hesitated for a moment before answering, wondering if it was worth saying anything. "I thought I was your friend, Emma. I thought we established that."

"We did."

"Then why haven't I heard from you in the past two days? You left and didn't say a word. That's not what friends do. You knew I would worry but that didn't seem to bother you. You just left." He pulled open the door and stepped outside.

"Let me at least explain," she said.

"No point. Glad you're okay," he mumbled and walked away, leaving Emma stunned. She closed the door, locked it, and turned off the hall light.

"Wonder what crawled up your ass?" she said to no one in particular, returning to the family room. She sat for a few moments, trying to watch another movie but lost interest as the image of Ryan kept resurfacing in her mind. She was unsure how she was going to deal with him. Yes, she could have phoned him sooner, but she shouldn't have to constantly check in with him. He needed to realize that she was capable of taking care of herself.

She decided to put it aside and go up to bed, her head heavy in thought. There was a lot to do in the next while. She tossed and turned for a bit before falling into a restless slumber.

"I'm so happy that you decided to move here," Julie Conners said to Emma. "Your mom would be happy, too. She thought you'd love it here."

Emma and Julie had arranged to meet for a quick meal at a local diner to catch up on things. She was thankful to still have a mother figure in her life, and Julie fit the bill well. Always thinking of others and always filled with love.

"I love what I see so far," Emma replied. "I think it's something I should have done years ago after Dad died. I could have taken care of Mom. Maybe she'd still be with us had I done that."

"Oh, stop that. You can't live by maybes. Put that right out of your head. You're here now and that's what counts." Julie stated.

"Well, thank you. One thing that made it easier for me to do this was the fact that you are here for support. You've been wonderful and I'm forever grateful."

"So, what are your plans. Are you looking for a job?"

"Not yet. I'd like to deal with all of Mom's things, get things off to charities that can use them. I'm a great believer that someone's discarded things can be someone else's treasures. I hate throwing good stuff into the trash and I'm not one for selling stuff when there are so many in need."

"If there's anything I can help with, you let me know. I may have a few things that I could add to what you give away." She finished off the last bite of the sandwich she had ordered and sipped her tea.

"That's great. There is one thing that you may be able to help me with." Emma said.

"What's that?"

"Mom wanted me to do something for the community in her name. I have a sizable amount to donate. I'd love some suggestions from you."

"You let me think about that for a bit."

"I had thought about donating funds to the cancer center in her name. I think she'd like that. They were so kind to her from what she has told me."

"Well, there you have it then. I think that's a wonderful idea. As a matter of fact, I think it should be announced at the tree lighting tomorrow. I'll get the CEO to be there to accept your donation. You are coming to that aren't you?"

"I was supposed to go with Ryan but he's more than upset with me right now. But, I'll try to be there. Although it's going to be a difficult time for me this Christmas, being the first without Mom, I do want to honor her. What time?"

"Six o'clock, but if you could be there about ten minutes early, I'll go through what's going to happen. Also, put a few words together addressing the community about your mom and her gift to the town."

"I've never had to give a speech before, but I'll try."

"Good. Now, what's wrong with Ryan?" Julie asked.

"I think he's upset that I didn't say anything to him before going home. Like I'm supposed to check in with him all the time because we're friends?"

"Oh, sweetie, don't you know he's in love with you? He's just wanting to make sure you are okay."

"He's not in love with me," she said adamantly. "Where did you get that? We've only known each other for a short time. It's not possible."

"Time has nothing to do with it. My Anthony and I, God rest his soul, fell in love right away. We were married six months after we met. You've heard of love at first sight, right? We were married for thirty years before he passed away," she stated proudly. "As for Ryan, he's been in a mood the last couple of days. I went to Lorenzo's for dinner Thursday night with a friend. Do you know Patti Goodwin?"

Emma shook her head indicating that she didn't.

"Anyways, Patti and I were having dinner and Lorenzo came over to chat. At one point, he asked if I had heard from Ryan. He stated that Ryan had been to the restaurant on

Wednesday, had a couple of drinks, complained about you not letting him know you were leaving, and then left depressed."

"Am I wrong Julie? He made it quite clear to me that he only wanted to be friends. And that's fine with me if that's all he wants, but friends don't expect their friends to account to them for everything they do. Yet he's expecting me to do just that. So why would he feel that way? Why do I have to account my time to him all the time? I'm a grown woman and I can take care of myself."

"He said he only wanted to be friends?" Julie asked surprised.

"Yes. Maybe in not in those exact words, but the meaning was clear."

"What exactly did he say?"

"He said he was fine on his own and that he didn't want or need another relationship. Then the other night, he said let's be friends."

"Dear girl, men are a constant wonder. Don't ever try to figure them out because they just aren't as complex as we think they are," she laughed. "If he said he's fine on his own, he means up until now he's been fine on his own. And the 'let's be friends,' well, doesn't every relationship start with a friendship? Don't read more into it than there is. Give the man a chance. I know he loves you and Lorenzo is of the same mind."

"Well, I'll just have to see what comes of it. We have some talking to do so that I can clear some things up with him. I was too tired to get into things with him last night when he showed up at my door. I'll keep you posted."

"You care about him, right?" Julie asked as she signaled the waiter for the bill. "I don't want to see him hurt. He's a good man."

"Yes, I care a lot for him," Emma said, a bashful smile on her face. "And I promise I'm not going to hurt him. He can only do that to himself." Emma finished her salad as the waiter came with the bill.

"I'm happy to hear that. Now, I have to get back. I have things I still need to do. I hope we can do this again. I've enjoyed getting to know you better and I promised your mom that I'd look out for you." Julie got up from her chair and Emma went over to hug her.

"Thank you again for the lunch. My treat next time. Maybe we can do this once a week, if you have time. I enjoy your company as well."

"That sounds lovely. You have a good day and I'll see you tomorrow, sometime before six."

"Oh, and I have this for you." She reached for the bag that was next to her chair. "Merry Christmas. You have a nice day, too."

"You didn't have to do that," Julie stated, taking the bag. "But thank you."

"It's a little something to say thank you for all that you've done for me." Emma had wrapped the robe and slippers that had been purchased for her mom, knowing that Julie would make good use of them.

Julie hugged her once more and Emma watched as she paid the bill and left.

Emma sat in front of her mother's closet in the bedroom, with the task ahead of her already playing on her emotions. It had been a week since her mother passed away and every once in a while, she still fell apart. She was comforted by the thought that her mom was without pain and with her father now. She had to believe that it was a better place for her.

Emma wasn't one to wallow in sadness, she got right to work on the tasks at hand. She knew that keeping busy was a good strategy to avoid emotional breakdowns. She pushed open the sliding door to see it stuffed full with clothes. She removed her mom's belongings out of the closet one by one, deciding what she wanted to do with the item. Keep it if it fits, give it away it if it doesn't, or throw it out if it isn't in good enough condition to donate. After the three-hour process of sorting through everything, she only kept a few things but was sure that there were going to be some very happy ladies when they received the clothes.

She then pulled open the dresser drawers and emptied them, spilling the items on the bed. She found the pajamas that she had given her mother last year for Christmas and remembered the bathrobe that she had purchased as a gift for this year.

Sadness took over for a moment, but she pushed through it and finished her sorting and moved on.

The donation pile was high. She tried to fold the clothes neatly so that they could be boxed up properly for transporting to Paula's House, where she decided to donate the clothes. She'd phone Julie to see if she had anything to add before packaging them up. She had done her research and found Paula's House to be the best choice. It was a place for women in need.

Emma went to the front entrance to check that closet. Coats and shoes were pulled out and carried to the bedroom, adding to the pile. She checked the office and the bedroom she was currently staying in and emptied those closets as well. It was well past dinner time by the time she was done, but she felt like she had accomplished something for the day.

While fixing herself something to eat, she pondered whether she should go to Ryan's to try and explain what had happened in the days before. Would he be receptive? She quickly finished her meal, cleaned up, and walked over to Ryan's house.

She stood for a moment at the front door wondering what she would say. Before she could ring the bell, the door opened. He looked surprised to see her standing there.

"Did you ring the bell? I didn't hear it," he said.

"I was just about to and then the door opened."

"Well, I'm on my way out. What can I do for you?"

"I wanted to explain what happened, Ryan. I deserve a chance to explain."

"But as I said, I'm on my way out. It will have to wait," he said as he stepped out, locking the door behind him.

"When then?" she asked.

"I'll try to come by when I get a chance. Sorry, I'm very late for a date." He walked past her, leaving her stunned for the moment. He got into his SUV and drove away. I guess that sums it up, she thought and returned home.

The more she reflected on it, the more miserable she became. She had hoped Julie and Lorenzo were correct in their opinions that Ryan was madly in love with her. Obviously not, she reasoned, if he's so eager to move on and date.

To her, the world had suddenly become a bleak place. She snuggled up on the sofa in the family room with a bottle of wine and a glass, feeling dejected once more, and watched movies. She couldn't help but feel that she jumped the gun by packing up her belongings in the city and moving into her mother's house, but now it was too late to do anything about that. The tears cascaded down her face, and there was nothing she could do to stop them. She missed her mom and wished she could turn back time. And she lost the one man that had finally broken through her tough shell. She drank the wine, trying to ease her troubled mind, and eventually fell asleep.

Chapter 15

At five in the morning, Emma awakened with the television still on and her body aching from not having slept in her own bed. She got up, turned off the television, and cleaned up the mess that had been left, cursing herself for wallowing in self-pity the night before.

After taking a hot shower that mostly alleviated her aches, she got ready for the day, ate a light breakfast, and jotted down a few remarks that she would be making to the public that evening regarding her mother's donation to the hospital's cancer clinic.

At nine o'clock, she left the house to go shopping for a few things and look for empty boxes that she might use to transport donations to Paula's House.

She returned home at eleven o'clock with boxes and food. She called Julie to see if she had anything to donate and informed her that she had decided to give everything to Paula's

House. Julie expressed her happiness with her decision and said she would be by shortly with her contribution.

"Please, come in," Emma greeted when Julie arrived.

"I didn't have time to go through all of my things but this is a good start." Julie replied, handing over the bags that she had brought.

"Would you like some coffee or tea?"

"A cup of tea would be lovely, thank you."

Emma placed the bags beside the boxes that she had brought down from her mother's room and set about making tea.

When Julie saw all the boxes, she gave an approving nod. "Paula will be happy to see all of these clothes come in. She gets many women through that house every year."

"Yes, I did some research--pregnant teens, women involved in domestic violence. It never would have occurred to me that there would be a need for a place like Paula's house in such a small town. It's a good thing she's doing for the women of this community. I'm sure she gets government funding, but I'm happy to help where I can. I think Mom would be pleased."

"I know she would be. She has donated there a few times over the years. You're doing a good thing."

"Thank you. I saw the weather report as I was checking my phone earlier, it calls for snow. The lighting goes on whether it's snowing or not, right?"

"Absolutely. It'll be a fresh white Christmas." Julie picked up the mug of tea that was put in front of her and took a sip. "You know, you are still welcome to have dinner with us tomorrow."

"Thank you for the offer, but I'm better off on my own this year. I don't think I'm going to be good company and I'd rather not bring anyone down during what's supposed to be a happy time with family. My life has changed so drastically in the last couple of weeks. I need to catch up with it," she said with a half-smile.

"I understand, but you are always welcome if you change your mind."

"Thank you."

"So, what's happening with Ryan?"

"Well, you and Lorenzo were definitely off the mark. He's not interested. I went over to try and explain why I left, but he wanted no part of it. He was actually on his way out when I went by. He told me he was late for a date."

"What? Who's he dating?"

"No idea but she must be something. He just left me standing there, got into his car, and drove away."

"That doesn't sound like him. There has to be a misunderstanding. Give it time, the truth will come out."

"I'm pretty sure I got the truth last night. So, I just need to do my own thing and move on. He's not the only fish in the sea."

"What's the matter with young people? You have to have trust in the people you care about. Everyone seems hurried and lazy. No one wants to take the time to stop, talk, and really listen anymore. It's no surprise that there are so many relationship problems with young people these days. "

"It's got to go both ways if it's going to work at all, Julie. That can't be one-sided."

"You're right. So have faith, and when the time is right, talk, stop, and listen, and all will be sorted out. I'm sure of it." Julie drank her tea and said goodbye, claiming she had more to accomplish before the tree lighting at six o'clock.

Emma packed the boxes into her car and drove over to Paula's House. She was surprised to see a young woman about her age answering the door.

"Hi, I'm here to see Paula," Emma stated.

"I'm Paula. May I help you?"

Emma did a quick study of the woman. Dark brown hair, tied back in a ponytail, clear complexion, green eyes, glasses, a wide nose and mouth with dimples. She wore a flannel shirt over jeans and slippers.

"Hello, Paula, nice to meet you. My name is Emma Jones. My mother has donated things to your cause in the past."

"Yes, Susan, wonderful lady. I'm sorry for your loss. Come in." Paula pulled the door wider to let Emma step in.

"Actually, I have a few boxes of things that I wanted to donate. Women's clothing. They were my mother's clothes. I thought I'd honor her by passing her things to you so that you can use them."

"That's wonderful. Do you need a hand?"

"I think there are six or seven boxes. Julie Conners also donated a few things. I can do it but it would go faster if you helped."

"Let me get my jacket and boots on and I'll be right out."

Emma stepped away from the door and went back to her car. She opened the trunk, pulled out a couple of boxes, and carried them to the door. By the time she went back for the next box, Paula was beside her. They emptied the car, carrying all the boxes inside.

"Can I offer you a cup of coffee or tea, or hot chocolate maybe?"

"I'd love a hot chocolate but some other time, if you don't mind. I'm supposed to be at the tree lighting and still have a couple of things that I'd like to do."

"I'll be there also. But feel free to drop in anytime. I'd be happy to show you what I do here."

"That would be great. I'd love to find out more. In the meantime, if I don't see you later, Merry Christmas." Emma turned to the door to pull it open.

"I think you've also probably given a few women here a Merry Christmas. Thank you for your kind donation and I'll be sure to thank Julie Conners also."

Emma left, feeling good about what she had just done and thought she'd like to know more about this woman.

Emma had gone home and wrapped Ryan's favorite painting, with the intention of giving it to him for Christmas as a thank you for everything he had done for her while her mother was so ill.

At 5:20 p.m., she left the house to walk to the tree lighting, bundled up to protect against the near zero-degree temperature. She stuffed the piece of paper in her pocket that contained the words that she was going to address to the community. It had just started snowing lightly, and there was no breeze, making it look magical. She stopped at the end of her driveway and took in the scene. It was dark, but the streetlights were on, and it seemed unusually quiet as no cars or voices could be heard. She looked up to the sky and let the snowflakes hit her face and realized that this could never be done in the city. Absolute silence had never been so wonderful. She glanced over her shoulder and noted that Ryan wasn't home and the sadness broke through her mood. She wished she was the one who'd captured his attention.

She was in awe of all the homes that were decorated with lights and displays as she strolled into town. It appeared as if everyone had taken special care to make their home look welcoming and beautiful for Christmas.

When she arrived, there was a sizable crowd that had gathered around the twenty-foot tree that was decked out with lights and ornaments of all different colors, shapes and sizes. The were all anticipating that special moment.

Emma spotted Julie at the small podium and went to her to discuss the speeches that were going to be made. She would be the third person.

"You nervous at all?" Julie asked.

"Not at all. I've never given a speach to a crowd of people before, but I don't mind public speaking and I have something good to say so that makes it easy. Did you get the CEO of the hospital here?"

"Yes, he's right over there," she said pointing to a young-looking man with a black coat, donning a fedora. "His name is Michael Winslow. We are almost ready to start. There is a chair for you back there if you want to sit," she responded, pointing to the small metal chair that had been set up.

Emma took a few steps back to let Julie do what she needed to do.

A few minutes later, Julie was at the podium talking to the crowd through a microphone that funneled into loudspeakers. She welcomed everyone to their 28th annual tree lighting ceremony and thanked the community for donating all the lights and ornaments. She introduced the town's mayor, who gave his speech about closing the old year with pride as the town had flourished, and going forward into the new year, there were new projects on the horizon to make the town a better place to live. When he was done, Julie introduced Emma.

Emma approached the podium, scanning the crowd who eagerly awaited her words.

"Good evening, everyone. Most of you don't know me. I am the daughter of Susan Jones, the owner of Giftable You. She had been living in this community for several years and loved it here, as did my dad while he was alive. My mom passed away nine days ago from cancer."

Julie watched the reaction of some of the women in front of her. There were tears and some pulling tissues from their pockets. The crowd was silent.

"I didn't get to spend much time with my mother before she died, but she told me about this amazing town called Willowbrook." The sentence was met with applause and cheers. "She hoped I would take over the house and relocate here to be a part of this wonderful community, a community that supported her and my father."

She spotted Katie in the crowd with a man that she could only assume was her husband.

"It was one of my mother's final wishes that I honor her and my father by doing something for the community." She noticed Ryan, he was smiling. He was with a woman who had her arm wrapped around his, and her heart sank. She looked away. *Push through it*, she reasoned. She continued, her attention fixed on the work at hand.

"At this time, I'd like to invite Mr. Michael Winslow up to the podium." Applause broke out as Emma waited for him to arrive before continuing. "Mr. Winslow, as CEO of the Willowbrook General Hospital, I'd love for you to accept this check," she pulled the check from her pocket, "from my parents' estate, for one hundred thousand dollars to be used for your cancer center." The crowd erupted in applause once again.

Michael Winslow smiled, extending his hand for a handshake and collecting the money she generously placed in his hand. He drew her in for a hug and thanked her.

Turning to the crowd, Michael made his own little speech. "Thank you, Emma, and thank you to your parents for their generous contribution. The cancer center is constantly in need of assistance, and this will undoubtedly help. As a small town, we are fortunate to have a hospital, and having a cancer center within the hospital is remarkable. Most small communities lack both. People in other little towns would have to go a considerable way to obtain the type of care that all of you can benefit from here. We are very fortunate to have it, as well as the exceptional folks who contribute year after year to keep it going. Thank you to everyone here for your generosity."

Julie joined them at the podium. "Well, let me just say this, Emma has already made great strides within the community. She also donated many things to Paula's House today. I've only known her for a short time but I'm impressed with her attitude of helping the community." Applause erupted once more. "I'm pleased to let you know that she has decided to be part of this community as she takes over her mother's house. I'd like you all to welcome her the way you would welcome family." More applause erupted.

"Before we light the tree, let me invite you all to stay, mingle, enjoy the hot chocolate and other goodies in the booths around us. Now, let's get to it, shall we?" Emma and Michael Winslow stepped away from the podium and the Mayor joined Julie. "If you would do the honors, Mayor."

The mayor stood in front of the crowd, looking at the anticipation on their faces. It was only a moment before he called out, "Merry Christmas everyone!" and pulled the lever that lit the tree.

The collective gasp from the audience as the tree lit up, said it all. Soon after, cheers erupted, and *O Christmas Tree* began to play over the loudspeakers and the crowd joined in singing. The lights flashed brilliantly, illuminating the giant tree, and the decorations glittered. The little snow that was still falling added to the enchantment of the event.

Emma was taken aback by the spectacle in front of her. She'd never witnessed anything like that before. Children's eyes widened, adults hugged, and the community that gathered together responded as if it were a family reunion.

She had fully expected the crowd to disperse after the tree was lit, but she was wrong. They stayed, they mingled, they drank hot chocolate, and enjoyed the treats being offered at the booths.

"You look surprised," a voice came from beside her. When she turned, she saw Michael Winslow approaching her.

"I am. I've never seen anything like this before," she replied with a smile.

"Yes, it is wonderful. I grew up with it so it's not the same for me as for you. I can't even imagine how it would feel to see all this for the first time."

"My mom said that living here is like living with family. It doesn't look like she was far off with that."

"Well, this one tops the cake but we do have other events that are close enough for comparison. You'll see it in the new year. I think the spring festival will delight you as well."

Emma saw Ryan and that girl approaching and didn't want to have to deal with that so she turned her full attention to Michael.

"So, aren't you pretty young to be CEO at a hospital?"

"Actually, yes, but I work hard and I'm recognized for that hard work and I've done well with the hospital. It's grown from a larger type of walk-in clinic to this wonderful place where our community can get the healthcare that they need. I'm great at raising money for what we need here."

"How long did it take you to build it up?"

"About fifteen years. In that time, I've raised about forty million dollars. The government kicked in, of course, paying about ninety percent of the construction cost. When it was built, we didn't have a cancer center. That was built about five or six years ago. I believe your mom was one of the first in the center after its construction. She always thanked me as it saved her traveling to the city for that kind of care."

"Well, I should thank you, too, then."

"Would you like some hot chocolate or maybe a coffee?"

"Sounds wonderful." As they slowly made their way to one of the booths, they were stopped a number of times by people that welcomed Emma to the community, thanking her for the donations. When they arrived at the booth, she was surprised to see that everything that was being offered was free. Emma picked up a coffee from the tray full of cups and Michael took from the hot chocolate tray.

"I don't drink hot chocolate often. Actually, I believe this is the only time I drink hot chocolate. Brings back Christmas memories for me," he chuckled.

Emma put back the coffee and picked up a hot chocolate as well. "Sounds like a tradition I want to start," she laughed.

"So, what does Emma do?" he asked as they started to wander around.

"Well, nothing right now. I just finished getting my stuff packed up in the city. It's on a truck, due here on Wednesday. I quit my job at Radison Industries, where I was a cost analyst, and have yet to decide what I'll do here."

"Cost analyst? How long have you done that kind of work?"

She laughed. "Too long, which is why it was easy to leave that position."

"Well, if you're looking for work, come and see me. I might have something for you."

"That's really kind of you but I'm not sure what I want to do at this point. I paint and have been told I'm good at it. I might be able to make a living doing something I love to do."

He stopped, looked at her. "I'd love to see your work. I was just mentioning to a colleague the other day, that we need new art in the halls of the hospital"

She wasn't sure what to make of the statement. Was this a come-on like many have done in the past or was he genuinely interested?

"Sure, I've brought some pieces with me. I didn't want to take the chance of them getting destroyed as I really like these. After the holidays, we can arrange something."

"Do you have family to spend the holiday with?" he asked.

"No, unfortunately," she said quietly, trying to keep her emotions in check. "I had hoped my mother would have survived to see Christmas one last time. I spent time dressing up the house for her but she never got to see it."

"I'm so sorry about your mom. I apologize for not expressing my condolences earlier."

"Emma?"

Emma turned to the voice, and seeing it was Katie, she pulled her in for a quick hug. "Hi, I'm glad you are here. I have something to tell you."

"This is my husband Jim." Katie said.

"Hi Jim. Nice to meet you." Turning her attention back to Katie she continued. "I stopped by the store and you were out. I was going to call you but I got wrapped up with my move here, sorry." She smiled at Katie, knowing that this would be the best Christmas gift she could give her. "I spoke with my lawyer and made arrangements to have the store put into your name if you want it."

Katie immediately hugged Emma. "I don't know what to say. How can I ever thank you for this?"

"Mom would have been happy to know that it's going to someone that cares about the business as much as she did. Merry Christmas, we'll get everything arranged before the new year."

"Merry Christmas to you too. And thank you again."

Emma turned and started to walk again with Michael by her side.

"That was very kind of you," he said.

"I have no interest in running a store. Mom said that if I didn't want it I could hand it over to Katie and with all the work that woman has put into that store over the last year, it's the least I could do."

"Still, very generous."

Sadness took over once more on the reminder she had just spoken of. "Thank you. You should get back to your family. They must be wondering where you are."

"No family. I'm on my own as well. I married when I was twenty-two and my wife died when I was twenty-five, which is why I started to raise money for a hospital. We couldn't get her to a hospital fast enough."

"I'm sorry to hear that. Now I understand why you dedicated your life to this."

"I don't want anyone else to go through that. Hospital care should be available immediately to anyone who needs it. I've spoken to other small communities over the years about what I went through and encouraged them to do the same. It's not easy but very gratifying in the end."

"I'm sure it is." She spotted Ryan nearby. Close enough for him to hear what they were talking about. He was alone now. She stopped and looked at Michael again. "Are you spending tomorrow with anyone?" she asked.

"No, as I said, I'm on my own. My parents moved to Florida and I'll go there in January for a visit, and my sister is in Europe with her family. I do Christmas alone most years."

"Well, why don't you stop by tomorrow for a coffee or tea, or maybe a hot chocolate, if you want, and I'll show you a few paintings."

"I'd love that." Emma gave him her address and then expressed how she was exhausted and wanted to go home.

"I'll drive you home if you want," he offered.

She accepted the offer and they left.

Ryan had overheard the exchange of the invitation to her house to view her artwork. Jealousy flashed through him like wildfire. She clearly didn't want anything to do with him if she was inviting other men into her home.

He had initially sought her out to speak with her. He saw she was chatting with Michael and didn't want to interrupt, so he waited for his turn. He needed to straighten out the misunderstandings with her once and for all. They needed to talk things out so that both understood each other's intentions.

Ryan mumbled to himself, "She's made that very clear now." No longer feeling like he wanted to be at the celebration of the tree lighting, he decided to go home. He had hoped earlier, to be walking home with Emma. It amazed him how quickly things changed.

As he was leaving, Lorenzo caught sight of him and stopped him. "Where are you going?"

"Home. Not in the mood for this."

"Why is that?"

"She's inviting other men to her house."

"Who?"

"Emma, who do you think?"

"She's back?"

"Yes, didn't you hear her speak earlier? She's back and she's still able to throw daggers into my heart without even trying."

"No, I didn't. I got here late and you owe me twenty bucks," Lorenzo said with a huge grin.

"What? What are you talking about?"

"The wager was that she'd be back before Christmas, remember?"

Ryan thought about it for a minute. "Yeah, I remember." He reached into his pocket, pulled out his wallet, and gave

Lorenzo the twenty that he owed him. "I'm going home now," he grumbled and left.

As he passed by her house, he noticed tire tracks in the driveway and only one pair of footprints leading inside the now-dark house. He knew Michael was a decent person, otherwise he would have stopped and warned Emma about him. He'd known Michael for a few years, had a few beers with him on a few occasions, and trusted him.

When he got home, he prepared for his visit with his family. A trip that he was no longer looking forward to. *But there's no point in staying here. I have to move on*, he thought.

When he had all his packages placed at the front door that he would be taking with him, he got himself a drink, lit the fire, and sat, thinking of Emma. He was happy when he heard that she was going to be moving to his little town, but it now posed a problem as well. He loved her and seeing her with another man wasn't something he could bear. How was he going to deal with it?

The doorbell chimed pulling Ryan from his thoughts. When he answered the door, he was surprised to see Emma standing there with a large gift wrapped package.

"Hi, come in," he said with a smile, stepping back to give her room.

"No, that's all right. I stopped by to give you this to say thank you for everything you have done for me since I've arrived. I appreciate it all."

"Please, come in. We need to talk." he said, taking the package from her extended hand.

"I'm tired Ryan. I need some sleep. I hope you have a Merry Christmas with your family. Please wish them a Merry Christmas from me." Emma turned to walk away.

"Emma. Stop. I know you're tired and so am I but we need to get some things sorted out," he called out.

"There's nothing to talk about right now," she said as she walked away. "Good night. Merry Christmas."

Frowning, Ryan watched her leave, then closed the door and carried the gift into the family room, leaning it up against the chair. He took another sip of his drink before unwrapping it.

As he pulled off the gift wrap and saw what it was, his heart burst. He placed the painting against the chair and sat on the sofa admiring it. Tears filled his eyes and ran freely down his face. It had meaning to him before, and now it had much more. Knowing that she painted this because of her father, had special meaning to her, and for her to give it to him made it that much more special to him.

He opened the envelope that was attached to it and read the Christmas card.

Ryan, wishing you a wonderful Christmas with your family. This is a small token in thanks for all that you did for me. Your support through the last days of my mother's life and thereafter was selfless and very much appreciated. I know you liked this painting. I hope it brings your heart some peace.

Merry Christmas

Emma

The urge to run over to her house to thank her, pull her into his arms and tell her how much he loved her was difficult to quell.

I need to do something before I leave in the morning, he though. She needs to know how much I appreciate what she's gifted me.

He sat for a few moments, staring at the painting, deep in thought about what he could do. He wiped the wetness from his face with the sleeve of his shirt as he got up to go to the small desk in the kitchen. Pulling a small thank you card from the desk drawer, he wrote:

Sweet Emma,

Words cannot describe how I'm feeling at this moment. The gift of the painting has filled me with emotions that I cannot easily define. I love it.

Thank you so much for this special gift. It means more than you could possibly know and will be treasured forever.

I hope that when I get back, we can take time to talk so that we can get some resolve to our current situation.

As difficult as it may be, I'm wishing you a peaceful Christmas.

Ryan

Ryan sealed the envelope, put on his boots and ran over to Emma's house. It was dark, all the lights had been turned off already indicating that she had, indeed, gone to bed. He placed the envelope in the mailbox and returned home.

Too tired now himself to think, and knowing that he had an early drive, he turned off the fire, the lights and went to bed.

Chapter 16

Emma watched Ryan from her mother's bedroom window, as he loaded his gifts and belongings into his SUV. She had gotten up early because she couldn't sleep and thought she'd go about packing up more of her mother's things, cleaning out the ensuite bathroom. She heard a car door close outside and went to the window. Peeking from behind the curtain, she saw Ryan.

She could feel the tears welling up in her eyes as he opened the driver's door to climb in behind the wheel. He took a brief look at his house, then her house and noticed her standing at the window on the upper floor. He tipped his head to the side as if perplexed as to why she was up so early. He hesitated momentarily, waved, and climbed into the SUV.

She watched him back out of his driveway and drive away. Overcome with sadness, she wasn't sure how she was going to make it through the day. It was Christmas morning, and she had no one to celebrate the day with. She longed for her mother.

Not wanting to wallow in self-pity, she grabbed one of the empty boxes she still had and took it into the ensuite along with a green garbage bag. She set about the task of emptying the vanity and the shelves behind the mirror. She took the time to thoroughly clean the bathroom and felt good about accomplishing something once it was done.

She stripped the linens off of her mother's bed and placed them into the laundry hamper, then removed the mattress off of the queen bed, leaning it up against the closet to be wrapped up. She retrieved some of her father's tools from the basement and proceeded to disassemble the bed, after snapping a picture of it. She would look around to see if it might be donated anywhere. She wrapped the pieces together, bagging the smaller ones so that they didn't get misplaced.

She then moved the mattress to the other side of the room giving her access to the walk-in closet. She cleaned the shelves and drawers, as well as vacuumed the carpet so that it was ready for when her belongings arrived. She then went into the main bathroom and emptied it of all of her mothers' belongings and cleaned it as well.

It was ten o'clock before she took a break. She went to the kitchen to make a pot of coffee, and stopped to turn on the tree lights in the living room. It was Christmas after all. But when she stood back to admire the tree, it was simply another reminder of her mother's absence from Christmas, and sadness consumed her once more.

She grabbed a mug of coffee and sat at the kitchen table with her computer, scanning through potential organizations where she might donate the furniture and other items.

Remembering an hour later that Michael would be stopping by to see her paintings later that day, she carried them down from her room upstairs, setting them up throughout the living room. When she finished that task, she pulled on her jacket and boots and went outside to shovel the driveway from the snow that had fallen through the night. She contemplated whether she should do Ryan's as well but decided against it.

She was ready when Michael arrived, having showered and dressed more presentably.

"Merry Christmas," he said as the door swung open.

"Merry Christmas to you as well. Come in," she said motioning with her hand. "Let me take your coat." While he removed his shoes, she hung his coat in the empty closet. "Welcome to my Mom's home."

"If you're going to continue to do that, it's going to take you much longer to get through the grieving stage," he expressed with concern. "It's your house now. How are you doing, by the way?"

"I'm fine. I still have my little pity parties, but all in all, I'm fine. I know she's with the man she loves and is no longer in pain. That helps."

"Yes, that would be the best way of looking at things. But the first holiday without a loved one is the hardest. It does get easier. I can tell you that."

"Can I offer you something to drink? Warm or cold."

"Coffee would be good, thank you."

Emma went into the kitchen to make a fresh pot of coffee and while it was brewing she showed him into the living room where her paintings sat.

"Wow," he exclaimed. "You are good. You've got some serious talent." He went to each painting studying them one by one, commenting on colors and style. They discussed brush strokes and the make of paints she used, even where she purchased her brushes. It made Emma's day to speak with someone that could appreciate her work. He spoke eloquently as if he knew what he was talking about, which made it more real for her.

"Thank you. I do have one more that I forgot to bring down. It's my mother's portrait. I painted it just after she passed away. It was my release and my way of remembering her."

"I'd love to see it," Michael said. "That is if it isn't too painful for you to show it."

"Come with me," she said and led him up the stairs. "Please, don't pay any attention to the condition of the upper floor. I'm trying to pack up my mom's things so that when the truck arrives on Wednesday with my things, I have room to put my belongings here."

When they reached the office, and she opened the door, the portrait of her mother stood on the easel where she had left it.

Michael gasped at the sight of it. "Emma, this is beautiful. What a way to remember your mother. She was a beautiful woman."

Emma's tears streamed down her face as she suddenly lost all control over them. She tried wiping them away so that he wouldn't notice but the action of it drew his attention.

"I'm sorry, Emma. I shouldn't have asked you to show me this. It's too soon."

Trying to make light of it, she tried to put on a smile. "I'm fine, really I am."

"What are you planning to do with the painting?"

Emma turned and headed back to the kitchen with Michael following. "I'm not sure yet. I wasn't thinking when I started it. It's a little too big to hang on any of these walls."

"Let me hang it in the Cancer Center with a plaque noting her contribution.."

The suggestion surprised her. She wasn't sure what to do, but the mere suggestion was admirable. "That's a wonderful offer. I'd like to think about it for a bit if you don't mind." They returned to the lower floor, she poured the coffee and suggested they go into the family room.

She turned on the fire and sat on the love seat while he got comfortable on the sofa.

"I can take you on a tour through the Cancer Center so that you could see what your mother has donated to. I think I have the perfect spot for her portrait, if you let me hang it." Michael commented as he sipped his coffee.

"I'd love a tour."

They chatted for a while about the Center, her mom and dad, and his family, and as the room darkened, they both realized that it was approaching dinner time.

"How about I treat you to dinner," he offered. "I'm getting hungry."

"I could fix you something,"

"No way. I'm not going to have you cook on Christmas Day for me. Let me treat you. We can go to Giovanni's or order in. Whichever you prefer."

"As much as I love Giovanni's, I'm sure he'd be closed today so let's just order in. I am famished as well."

They quickly decided where they were ordering from and what they wanted, and it was delivered within the hour. Emma turned on the television when the meal arrived, and they watched *National Lampoon's Christmas Vacation* movie as they ate, laughing throughout it.

When the movie ended, Michael thanked her for her company. "Christmas wasn't as bad this year. I thank you for that." He got up to leave.

"And I thank you for giving me a reason to laugh today. You made it easier for me as well."

He walked to the front door, put on his shoes and pulled his coat from the closet. "Let me know when you want that tour of the center." He reached into his back pocket for his wallet, retrieved his card and handed it to her. "Call me when you are ready."

"I will, thank you. I enjoyed your company and thank you for dinner," she smiled.

He turned, opened the door and stepped out. "Good night, Emma. I had a good time."

"Good night," she responded and closed the door.

Ryan had just pulled into his driveway, and saw Michael getting into his car. He stayed in his vehicle and watched as Michael drove away and wondered if he should go and talk to her now.

He weighed the pros and cons of it and decided for his own sanity, he'd try.

He carried his belongings into his house before going to hers. He his gift for her from his bedroom and pulled the gift from his parents to her from the bags of things he had just brought in from the car.

When he rang her doorbell she opened the door saying "Did you forget something?" Upon seeing him, she felt a little embarrassed. "Merry Christmas," she said. "Sorry, I thought you were someone else."

"Yeah, I know, Michael. I watched him leave."

Her guard went up right away. *Is he watching me?* "What do you want Ryan?" she asked in a cold tone.

He could feel the mood change. He was concerned that he made a mistake. "I came give you these gifts and to talk with you."

"I'm tired, can we talk some other time?"

"No, I think we need to talk now."

She motioned him inside as she stepped back from the door. "Okay, talk to me."

"Emma, please," he begged, "let's sit down and have a real conversation."

"Oh, all right. I'm going to get some wine. Would you like a drink?"

"I'll join you with a glass of wine if you have enough."

"You go into the family room, I'll be back with the wine." She went into the kitchen to get a bottle from the fridge and two wine glasses.

"All right," she said, setting the bottle and glasses onto the coffee table. "What do you want to talk about?"

Ryan had placed the gifts on the coffee table, picked up the bottle, opened it, and filled the two glasses. "Emma, clearly something is going on between the two of us. I don't know what happened but we went from being friends to this rift between us. I don't understand it. I don't understand what happened or how it happened."

"Ryan, you said you wanted to be friends. I accepted that but that doesn't mean I need to check in with you whenever I do something or go somewhere. You got angry with me because I didn't tell you I was going to the city. I don't need to account to you for my time." She sipped her wine.

"You're right. You shouldn't have to account to me for your whereabouts, but I was worried about you. You just disappeared. Why wouldn't I be worried? You just lost your mother, you're grieving, and you just disappeared."

"I asked Julie to let you know where I was going."

"She forgot but when I called her, she told me. But why didn't you answer my calls? You could have done that. It would only have taken you a moment to tell me what was going on." He could feel his voice getting a little louder than he wanted.

"I couldn't. My phone dropped and broke. It took me a while to get another one." She took another gulp of her wine. "Ryan, I wanted to explain everything to you but you were in a hurry to get somewhere."

"Yeah, I remember, but I'm here now. So, explain, why don't you," he said raising his eyebrows and crossing his arms.

"Well, I'm not sure I'm liking your attitude right now," she replied raising her voice a little to match his. "Explaining was something I was going to do as a courtesy. It's not something I'm obligated to do and you sit here almost demanding an explanation." She stood, waiting for his reply, knowing that if she didn't like it, she would see him out the door.

Ryan took a moment to let things settle before they got heated to a point of no return. "I'm sorry, that wasn't my intention." He sipped at his wine and continued. "You don't owe me an explanation and I guess I'm just frustrated with this whole situation."

Emma sat down again. "Ryan, I'm just as frustrated, and honestly, I don't know what to do about it. You said you wanted to be friends and I'd like that but know the limits that go with that."

"And what if I want more?" he asked.

"I don't understand. You said you were fine on your own, then you tell me you were late for a date. I see a woman draped around you at the tree lighting and you sit here and tell me you want more?"

"Let me…"

"No, no need to explain," she started, cutting him off. "You made it very clear to me many times now. Friendship is what you wanted. I don't want to be a sidekick if you are dating someone else." She got up once more. "Now, please leave. I think enough has been said," she stated with tears running down her face.

Ryan got up and went to her. "Look at me, Emma," he started.

"No, just go. I'm tired and this just isn't the best time to get things said. I'd be saying things that I don't mean if we keep going."

Understanding what she meant with that, with emotions being strained, running high, he chose to let it go for now and go home. "I'm sorry, Emma. I've never intended to upset you. I'll go but please, let's sit and talk tomorrow and if not then, let's do it soon. I really think there are a lot of misunderstandings here."

"I just can't do this anymore tonight," she said looking at him with tears running down her face. "Now, please go. I'm tired."

He hesitated, saw the pain on her face. He wished he could pull her in and hug her. He wished he could make all that pain go away for her. But again he was wrong with his timing and instead of doing what he wanted to do, he left with a heavy heart, letting himself out, leaving her crying in the family room as he closed the door. He checked the mailbox and saw that his note had not been found yet, disappointing him more.

When Emma heard the front door close, she went to it, locked it, and turned off the hall light. She sat in the family room with the fire going, and cried. She thought about all that he had said. And when that attitude of his kicked in, she just felt crushed.

Why doesn't he understand that he can't have things both ways? Why doesn't he understand that I am self-sufficient and don't need him to do everything for me? Why is he expecting so much from me? It just isn't fair.

She sipped for the glass of wine that he poured, going over the conversation.

Enough is enough, it's time to move on. I'll go about doing what I want to do and to hell with him. I don't need more heartache.

Emma cleaned up the family room, gifts untouched and turned off everything in the lower level of the house. She went up to the office and sat in front of her mother's portrait, silently holding a conversation with her. She remembered her mothers words before she died and closed her eyes, listening for her voice. She so desperately needed to hear her speak and when she was ready to give up, she sensed her mother with her. She could feel the warmth of her mother's touch as she felt arms embracing her and then heard the words, 'be patient, it will all work out.' She quickly opened her eyes and looked around as it seemed so real. Had it not been for the fact that she saw her mother being put into the ground, she would have thought her mom was here, in the same room with her now.

But as soon as she opened her eyes, the feeling of being embraced was gone. Her mother was gone again, but she knew she had been blessed with that moment.

"Thanks mom. I needed that."

Chapter 17

Emma woke up with a 'to hell with men' attitude on Monday morning. She wasn't going to let Ryan spoil what she wanted while living in this small town. She spent the next couple of days getting the house ready for the arrival of the movers. She had taken down the Christmas tree and stored it and all of the ornaments in the basement. She removed some of the pictures from the walls around the house that she no longer wanted, emptied bookcases and cupboards of items she no longer needed, and sifted through everything in the basement, emptying the house of more than half its contents.

It was a difficult job, to be sure, and she had her mini-breakdowns throughout the days when she came across items that meant something to her mother or father. She moved items into the garage, assuring herself she'd figure out what to do with everything.

There was a lot more space for her belongings by the time the movers arrived on Wednesday.

Emma instructed the movers to stack the boxes in the living room so that she could sift through them from there. She thanked them and tipped them generously when they were finished. Before closing the door, she pulled the mail from the mailbox and dropped it on the kitchen table without looking at it. She knew that the bills would be rolling in, and she would deal with them at some point. But for now, they could wait.

She wasn't in a hurry to get things unpacked as she wanted to do some renovations first. Now that the stores were open, she felt it was time to shop for what was going to make her comfortable in her home.

She spent hours over the next few days, contacting painters, and flooring people, each dropping in with samples and some leaving with instructions and contracts for the upcoming days. She ordered furniture that was to be delivered in the new year. She hired movers to pack up her mother's furniture and move it to the thrift warehouse on the other side of town.

She had informed the proprietors of the thrift store that anybody in desperate need of furniture would be allowed to claim pieces for free, and they had agreed. She bought new curtains and rugs, and by the end of the day, she knew she'd have a better-suited house by the end of January. The only thing that she knew she had left to do was the renovation of the kitchen, but that could wait, she thought.

During that time, she didn't hear from Ryan, but Michael had called her a number of times. He dropped by a couple of times in the evening to take her out for dinner or order in and watch a movie.

He had also arranged a tour of the Cancer Center in the hospital so that she could see where her mother's portrait might hang. She was pleased with the location that he had chosen, on the wall directly in front of the entrance for everyone to see.

"It's a perfect spot. Thank you, Michael."

Michael was pleased that she was happy and wrapped his arms around her, pulling her in for a kiss.

Emma was instantly aware of what was about to take place, pulled away and took two steps back. "I'm sorry, Michael, I'm not ready for an involvement right now. I've just lost my mother, I've had my heart broken, and I just need time to figure out me again. I'd love to remain friends though. I enjoy your company."

"Emma, I completely understand and frankly, I shouldn't have even tried. I know your heart is with Ryan. Everyone sees it but the two of you."

"Well, that's not going to happen," she responded.

"I'd want to remain friends. Let's see what the new year brings."

Michael arranged for the painting to be picked up and framed and told her he would invite her back, once it was hung.

While Emma was busy organizing the changes needed in the home, Julie was plotting a plan with Lorenzo at the Giovanni's. She had spotted Emma with Michael one evening as they entered a restaurant on Main Street. Her concern led her to Lorenzo, hoping he could help get Emma back with Ryan.

"I don't know what to do with these two young people. How on earth are we going to get them in the same room again, let alone have a life together?"

She had explained what Emma had told her and he, in turn, told Julie about his conversations with Ryan. "They are both in love and they are both stubborn as hell. Ryan does have a way of putting his foot in his mouth every so often. He's a good man, though," Lorenzo stated.

"Yes, he is. And I know that Emma loves him. But for some reason, she believes that he's dating and just wants to be friends, have her as a sidekick, as she put it."

"And he believes that she's not interested. Only wants to be friends. That she's dating other men. Michael was a name that came up."

"What are we going to do?"

Lorenzo poured her a cup of tea when the tea arrived at the table. He had something much stronger. "We have to have a party and then find a way to put them in a room together where they can't get out."

"What, you're just going to lock them up?" she laughed.

"If that's what it takes. A New Years' party. It's short notice but I think it can be arranged. What if I set aside one of my private rooms, set it up for a dinner. I'll invite each to a New Year's dinner stating that I would like to have dinner with them. When they get here, I'll escort them personally to the room and then lock them in for a few hours. They won't have a choice but to talk."

"Well, I think that sounds like a plan. What can I do to help?"

"I'll call both and let you know if they accept or not. If not, I'm going to count on you to convince them to go. They won't know the other will be there. I'll take care of everything else."

"Let's hope this works. I can't bear to see either of them hurting anymore. Poor Emma has been through so much lately.

She's digging in, keeping herself so busy that she doesn't have time to think about anything when it comes to Ryan. I think she's actually given up hope."

"We'll fix that. It's hard watching my friend go back under. Eight years ago when he lost his wife, he was in bad shape. He's not much better now. Let's call now."

Lorenzo pulled his phone from his pocket and dialed Ryan's number. "Hello, my friend, how are you?" he said in a cheerful voice. He listened for a bit and then spoke to Ryan again. "I'm sorry to hear you're in the dumps. Why don't you come here for dinner with me on New Year's Eve? I'd love to sit and chat with you. Have a good steak, a couple of drinks, and we can wish for a better year together. How does that sound? You can even join the party here after dinner. I'm closing the restaurant for food at nine o'clock and I'll be hosting a New Year's eve party. What do you think?"

He listened for the response again and then replied. "Wonderful, I'll see you about six o'clock then on Saturday. Dress nice, I run a classy place." He disconnected the call. "One down, one to go."

He punched in the number that Julie gave him and put her on speaker phone when she answered.

"Hello?"

"Hello, sweetheart, how are you doing?"

"I'm fine, who is this?"

"This is your favorite chef."

"Hello, Antonio, how did you get my number?"

"I'm insulted," Lorenzo replied.

Emma laughed. "I know it's you, Lorenzo, and you *are* my favorite chef. I just wanted to see how you'd react. How are you?"

"My heart it still hurts."

"How can I make it up to you?"

"Have dinner with me. New Year's Eve. I'll fix a nice steak for you, a couple of drinks, and lots of talking, how does that sound?"

"Sounds wonderful. I'd really like that."

"Good, then I'll see you at 6:15 on Saturday."

"I'll be there, thank you, Lorenzo."

"You're very welcome my dear. Looking forward to it. Dress up for me, it's New Year's Eve."

"I will, gives me a chance to wear some of my nice clothes. Looking forward to it as well." And the call was disconnected.

Julie laughed. "That couldn't have played out any better. You're not only a great chef but a genius as well."

"Thank you, my dear lady. Now I just have to work out the little details."

"You let me know what I can do to help."

"Well, there might be one thing. If you could find a way to delay Emma so that she doesn't actually arrive until after six-thirty, that would take my fear of both arriving at the same time away."

"Oh, I'm sure I can manage that. Leave it to me." She grinned and stood up. "Time for me to go. Thank you for being so good about this but I think they need that helping hand. They are perfect for each other and the only ones that don't see that are them."

"I agree." Lorenzo walked her to the door and helped her on with her coat. "If you have no plans New Year's Eve, come by after nine and I'm sure we will have lots to celebrate. Drinks on me."

She gave him a hug. "Sounds wonderful."

He opened the door for her, and she left feeling blessed for having such a good friend.

Chapter 18

Ryan took his time getting ready for dinner with Lorenzo. He was looking forward to the after-party as well. Emma would no longer be someone he pursued. Her attention had obviously shifted to Michael. He'd seen them together a few times before, and each time it shattered his heart as they talked and laughed together.

Knowing that the only way to go on was to find someone else, and now that he was ready to do that, he banked on Lorenzo's customary gatherings, which normally drew a large number of women. He'd meet up with someone for the evening, he reasoned, and he'd attempt to have a good time, he thought, and then realized that doing anything without Emma was going to be difficult.

Ryan hadn't worn his blue pinstriped suit in a while, but Lorenzo had told him to dress up. He took a shower, trimmed his beard to resemble a five o'clock shadow, applied his favorite cologne, and fixed his hair, finishing with a dab of gel to keep it in place.

He studied his reflection in the mirror for final approval, and his mind went to Emma once more, wondering how she would be celebrating the arrival of the New Year.

The white shirt and navy and white tie added the classy look for which he was striving. He took his good shoes from the closet and examined himself in the mirror after putting on his navy socks. He wasn't satisfied with his receding hairline and observed a touch of gray, but he was pleased with the overall look.

At ten minutes to six, he hopped into his SUV and drove to Giovanni's. When he stepped through the door, Lorenzo was waiting for him and took him to the bar for a drink.

Emma had showered and fixed her hair and makeup before stepping into her red strapless gown. She had seen the gown in a boutique window in the city and couldn't resist purchasing it for that 'just in case' occasion years ago. This was as good of an occasion as any.

She took a 10k gold necklace with a diamond pendant from her jewelry box and put it on.

Her mother had given it to her when she purchased the condo. A celebratory gift. She had found matching earrings years later and bought them for the overall look with the necklace. When she examined herself in the mirror, she was pleased to see the reflection.

She heard a knock on the front door and when she answered it, she was surprised to see Julie.

"Oh, my," Julie said, putting her hands to her cheeks. "You look absolutely stunning. Where are you off to?"

"Come in, don't stand out there in the cold." Emma replied. "I'm going out for dinner and was told to dress up. Being New Year's Eve, I went all out," Emma giggled. "Do you think it's too much?"

"Not at all. I think it's a wonderful time to go all out. New Year's happens but once a year. Celebrate."

"I plan to. Thank you. What brings you by?"

"I thought I'd invite you to my house if you weren't doing anything. I have a couple of people coming over to bring in the New Year. Thought you might like to join us. But, I see you have other plans. Who's taking you to dinner?"

"Lorenzo invited me. It was very sweet of him."

"Great, I hope you are staying for the New Year's Eve party he has every year. I'm sure there will be lots of people there that you can meet."

"I'll only stay if he wants me to. He never mentioned the party."

"Well, you can't let a dress like that go to waste. Make sure you get an invite from him," she smiled and checked her watch. It was twenty past six and safe to let Emma go. "You call me tomorrow and let me know how things went. If you get home early, come join us. You know where I am."

"I'll do that. I have to go now, I was supposed to have been there five minutes ago. Thanks for coming by with the invitation." She gave Julie a hug and watched her leave. She grabbed her evening purse, put on her coat, and drove to Giovanni's.

"Come, let's get you some food." Lorenzo led Ryan into a small room that had but one table in it, dressed with white linens and a flower centerpiece with candles. The room had a small fireplace in the corner and the lights had been dimmed.

"Ah, should I be worried?" Ryan asked as he stepped into the room. "Are you making a play for me?" he laughed.

"Hey," Lorenzo stopped, pointing a finger at Ryan. "Know to whom you are talking to. I don't do men." Lorenzo looked shocked and then laughed. "The room had been reserved for a special couple but there was a change of plans. I thought this way we can talk freely without busybodies listening."

"You had me worried for a bit." Ryan laughed.

Lorenzo had Ryan sit with his back to the door, and he sat in the other chair. "Oh, wait, I have to get something. I'll be right back." He got up, lit the candles, "I love candles, what can I say," and stepped out of the room, closing the door behind him.

While Lorenzo went to the front door, awaiting the arrival of Emma, a waiter had stepped into the room where Ryan was, taking his order and leaving again. Ryan pulled out his phone and scrolled through social media accounts.

"Emma, I've never seen anyone so beautiful," Lorenzo exclaimed when she stepped through the front door and removed her coat. He studied her from top to bottom, admiring the slim figure that was wrapped in a red gown, cinched at the waist and flowing straight down with a side split to the upper thigh. He took her hand, lifting it high above her and gave her a twirl. "Magnifico!" He kissed her on both cheeks and gave her a hug.

"Thank you, Lorenzo, you did say get dressed up."

"And I'm now very happy I said that," he smiled. "Come, let's get some food." He led her down the hall, past other rooms that were occupied with other diners to a room where the door was closed. He waited a moment for his waiter to arrive.

Emma was surprised that the waiter would be entering the room with them but as soon as the door opened, she understood what was going on.

Lorenzo guided Emma to the other side of the table where Ryan sat, pulled out the chair and asked her to sit.

"Lorenzo, you disappoint me. I thought we were having dinner together. I'm not sitting here with Ryan as I have no intention on having an uncomfortable evening. I'm sorry."

Ryan stood up. He couldn't help but notice how stunningly beautiful she was. He could feel the heat rising in the room. "I'm just as disappointed in you, my friend. I don't know what you were thinking but this is definitely your biggest mistake. I'm leaving." Ryan turned to leave but Lorenzo stopped him at the closed door.

As the waiter put the food on the table, Lorenzo pleaded his case.

"You both are my two favorite people. I care about both of you. I've seen how happy you can be together and I've watched as you've both become miserable because of misunderstandings. If both of you can get through this meal, talking to each other, trying to straighten things out, I'll never pry again. But I need both of you to put in an effort."

Ryan looked back at Emma who was dazzling. How could he not try? "All right, I'll give it a go if you will, Emma. You look stunning, by the way." He flashed his crooked smile at her.

That smile was all she needed to melt her heart. He had never looked better, and she could feel the pull of attraction. "Fine. I'm starving anyways, and can't think of a better plase to eat. So, let's eat," she replied.

"I'll be back with the wine. Sit, talk, be kind," Lorenzo said with a smirk on his face, before he stepped out the door.

Ryan approached her and pulled out her chair. As she sat down, he caught the aroma of her perfume and the scent captivated him. He had always thought she was beautiful, but tonight, she had absolutely won his heart.

He knew that Lorenzo was right, and he was determined to rectify the situation between them. He rounded the table to take his seat as a waiter came in with a bottle of white wine. He filled the two glasses and set it on the table and stepped out of the room, closing the door behind him.

"Did you get my note?"

"What note would that be? I didn't get anything."

"Weird, I put it in your mailbox. It was a thank you note for the painting. It's special. I know you painted it when your dad passed away. I'm sure it means something to you."

"Yes, but you liked it, and I wanted a special way to say thank you to you, for all that you've done for me."

"It was very sweet of you to do that Emma. I'll treasure it forever, thank you."

"There were some things in my mailbox, but I just dumped it all on the kitchen table. I haven't gotten to it all yet. I thought it was just bills for my mother."

"I understand. I'm sorry, Emma. I had no idea that Lorenzo would do this. "

"Not your fault. I don't blame you," she said, lifting her wine glass and taking a sip. "How were you to know?"

"My parents send their love. Did you open their gift?"

"Actually, no. I didn't know the gift was from them and to be honest, I wasn't in the right frame of mind to open gifts, but thank them for me. Or, better yet, I'll give them a call tomorrow to thank them myself."

"There was a gift there from me too. I guess you didn't open that one either," he went on. "I understand."

"Sorry, should have opened them. Thank you for thinking of me and leaving me a gift. I'll open it tomorrow."

There was a pause that was heavy. An uncomfortable moment before she spoke again. "So, how are you?"

"Absolutely miserable," Ryan replied. "I've missed you. I've missed our time together."

"I've missed you, too. It's really hard losing a friend, especially after losing a mother."

"Seems like you've moved on already though," he said.

"What do you mean?"

"Michael. The two of you seem to be hitting it off. He's a good man. If he makes you happy, then I'm happy for you."

"Michael is a friend. Only a friend." She cut into her steak, putting a piece into her mouth. "Oh my God, this is absolutely the best steak I've eaten."

Ryan cut his steak and put it into his mouth and nodded in agreement. "This reaffirms my friendship with him," he laughed. Emma couldn't help but laugh with him.

He saw the way her face lit up when she laughed and smiled. "Emma, can we go back and talk about what happened. I'm so confused. I need to get it all out on the table so that I understand what happened so that I can try to fix things."

"I'd like that, too. Maybe once it's all said, we can then decide if we want to be friends again."

"Emma, I told you I want more. I want to be more than just friends."

"Why, Ryan?" Emma questioned with the sudden oncoming of frustration once again. "The woman you were with isn't enough?"

"The woman I was with? What woman? Who are you talking about?"

"The one draped across your arm at the tree lighting. The one you were meeting when you told me you were late for a date," she stated. "And, why would you say you want more when you clearly told me you were fine on your own?" She looked down into her food, suddenly not hungry anymore.

"Look at me, Emma," he said. And when she didn't look up, he continued. "I'm not dating anyone. The woman I was meeting the other day and who was draped around me at the tree lighting was my cousin. I haven't seen her in years. She was passing through town with her husband on their way to the city. He was standing on the other side of her at the tree lighting but I'm sure you didn't notice him."

He got up and went to her when he noticed the tears. He pulled her up and gently wiped the tears away. "And yes, I'm good on my own. I can survive. I have survived, but I know I'd be better with you. And yes, I want friendship because if you can't be friends in a relationship, you can't be anything else."

"I'm so confused, Ryan. I don't know what you want from me."

"Do you care about me at all?" he asked, lifting her face gently so that she was looking into his eyes.

"Yes, of course, I do," she replied meekly.

A huge smile appeared on his face as he hugged her, and silently thanked God that everything was now going the way that he had wanted it previously. When he stepped back, he looked into her eyes, and he said the words that he had been hoping to have the chance to say for quite some time now.

"I love you, Emma Jones. I know it's fast, but I've never felt quite like this before. I never believed in love at first sight but this comes damn near to it. I've wanted to tell you that for a while now. When I saw Michael leave Christmas day, I knew I couldn't wait any longer which is why I came over to talk to you. But you made it clear to me that you were done with me. It hurt deeply."

"Oh, Ryan. Michael means nothing to me. We spent Christmas together because we were both alone. He came to see my paintings. That's all," she replied.

He waited, hoping to hear the words back. He hugged her once more, kissing the top of her forehead.

She pulled back a moment later. "Ryan, I have struggled with my feelings about you for a while now. It's been a bit of a roller coaster ride emotionally. Partly because of my mom's passing, but also because I never believed you could fall in love so quickly. I love you, too."

He didn't need to hear anything else. His heart warmed as he lightly brushed his lips against hers, testing the reaction and when she pulled him closer, he kissed the lips of the woman he wanted to spend the rest of his life with, and she melted into his embrace.

The End

ABOUT THE AUTHOR

I was born and raised in Toronto, Ontario. I am happily married and have two children, two step-children, and five grandchildren, all of whom I don't see often enough.

My passions are family time, traveling around the world, lying on a beach, reading romance stories, and photography.

I became passionate about writing since the start of Covid 19 in 2020. It has become a way for me to voice my thoughts and feelings, where I'm normally an introvert and quiet when around others. I have many stories running wild in my head that I can't seem to get down on paper fast enough.

I hope you enjoy what's to come. :)

Other Books

Romantic Mystery Series – with a touch of steam

The Cross Link– Series Prequel
Book 1 – Never Call Me Sweetheart

Coming Soon:

The Cross Link Series
Book 2 – Crazy Without You

Contemporary Romance
The Beach Cottage

Visit my website and sign up for the newsletter to keep up-to-date with new books and release dates.

https://www.authordianakurth.com/

PLEASE LEAVE A REVIEW

Thank you for taking the time to read this book. I hope you liked it.

I would be grateful if you could please leave a review on Amazon and/or GoodReads.

Authors depend on reviews to gain readership.

Made in the USA
Middletown, DE
30 November 2022

16522454R00161